Henry Inman

The ranche on the Oxhide

A story of boys' and girls' life on the frontier

Henry Inman

The ranche on the Oxhide
A story of boys' and girls' life on the frontier

ISBN/EAN: 9783337142933

Printed in Europe, USA, Canada, Australia, Japan

Cover: Foto ©Andreas Hilbeck / pixelio.de

More available books at **www.hansebooks.com**

THE RANCHE ON THE OXHIDE

·The· M C͗o ·

"The most indescribable antics were gone through."

THE RANCHE ON THE OXHIDE

A STORY OF

Boys' and Girls' Life on the Frontier

BY

HENRY INMAN

LATE CAPTAIN UNITED STATES ARMY
BREVET LIEUTENANT COLONEL

AUTHOR OF "THE OLD SANTA FÉ TRAIL"

SIX FULL-PAGE ILLUSTRATIONS

New York

THE MACMILLAN COMPANY

LONDON: MACMILLAN & CO., LTD.

1898

Norwood Press
J. S. Cushing & Co. — Berwick & Smith
Norwood Mass. U.S.A.

To My Grandson

GEORGE INMAN SEITZ

CONTENTS

CHAPTER I

CHAPTER II

CHAPTER III

CHAPTER IV

CHAPTER V

CHAPTER VI

CHAPTER VII

CHAPTER VIII

CHAPTER IX

CHAPTER X

CHAPTER XI

CHAPTER XII

CHAPTER XIII

CHAPTER XIV

CHAPTER XV

CHAPTER XVI

CHAPTER XVII

CHAPTER XVIII

CHAPTER XIX

CHAPTER XX

CONCLUSION

ILLUSTRATIONS

xiii

THE RANCHE ON THE OXHIDE

———∘∘⟩⊙⟨∘∘———

CHAPTER I

IN 1865–66, immigrants began to rush into
the new state of Kansas which had just been
admitted into the Union. A large majority
of the early settlers were old soldiers who had
served faithfully during the war for the preser-
vation of their country. To these veterans the
Government, by Act of Congress, made certain concessions, whereby they could take up
"claims" of a hundred and sixty acres of the
public land under easier regulations than other
citizens who had not helped their country in
the hour of her extreme danger.

B   I

Many of them, however, were forced to go out on the extreme frontier, as the eastern portion of the state was already well settled. On the remote border several tribes of Indians, notably the Cheyennes, Kiowas, Comanches, and Arapahoes, still held almost undisputed possession, and they were violently opposed to the white man's encroachment upon their ancestral hunting-grounds, from which he drove away the big game upon which they depended for the subsistence of themselves and their families. Consequently, these savages became very hostile as they witnessed, day after day, the arrival of hundreds of white settlers who squatted on the best land, felled the trees on the margin of the streams to build their log-cabins, and ploughed up the ground to plant crops.

Late in the fall of 1866, Robert Thompson, a veteran of one of the Vermont regiments, having read in his village newspaper such glowing accounts of the advantages offered by Kansas to the immigrant, decided to leave his ancestral homestead among the barren hills of the Green Mountain State, and take up a claim in the far West. The family, consisting of father, mother,

Joseph, Robert, Gertrude, and Kate, after a journey by railroad and steamboat without incident worth recording, arrived at Leavenworth on the Missouri River, the general rendezvous in those early days for all who intended to cross the great plains, through which a railroad was then an idle dream. In that rough, but busy town, Mr. Thompson purchased two six-mule teams, two white-covered wagons called "prairie schooners," together with sufficient provisions to last a month, by which time he thought he should find a suitable location on the vast plains whither he was going.

A few cooking-utensils of the simplest character, together with a double-barrelled shot-gun and a Spencer rifle, constituted the entire outfit necessary for their lonely trip of perhaps three hundred miles, before they could hope to find unoccupied land on which to settle.

One Monday morning, bright and early, the teams pulled out of the town, Mr. Thompson driving in the lead, and Joe, who was the elder of the boys, in the other. Gertrude rode with her father and mother, and Kate and Rob with their brother Joe. Their course ran over the broad trail to the Rocky Mountains, on which were then hauled by government caravans, all the supplies for the military posts in the Indian country.

Their route for the first two weeks passed through deep forests extending for a long distance from the bank of the great river. The whole family were charmed with the new and strange scenes they passed as they rode slowly on day after day, scenes so different in their details from those to which they had been used in the staid old region they had left so far behind them. The boys and girls, particularly, were in a constant state of excitement. They marvelled at the immense trees as they passed through groups of great elms and giant cotton-woods. The gnarled trunks were vine-covered clear to their topmost branches by the magnificent Virginia creeper, or woodbine, as it is called, the most beautiful of the American ivies, and which grows in its greatest luxuriance west of the Missouri River. On the ends of the huge limbs of the lofty trees as they branched over the trail, the red squirrels sat, peeping saucily at the travellers as they drove under them, and the blue jay, the noisiest of birds, screeched as he darted like lightning through the dark foliage. The blue jay is the shark of the air; he kills, without any discrimination, all the young fledglings he can find in their nests while their parents are absent. Although his plumage is magnificent in its cerulean hue as the sun glints upon it, and he has a very sweet note when sitting quietly on the limbs of the oak, which he loves, yet his awful screaming as he flies — and he is ever on the wing — is far from pleasant to ears not trained to listen to his harsh voice.

Occasionally a gaunt, hungry wolf—they are always hungry — would skulk out of the timber and then run across the trail, with his tail wrapped closely between his legs. He would just show a mouth full of great white teeth for a moment, as he sneaked cowardly off, the rattle of the wagons having, perhaps, disturbed his slumbers on some ledge of rock near the road.

Prairie chickens, or pinnated grouse, were seen in large flocks as soon as the open country was reached. They were far from wild in those days; you could approach near enough always to get a good shot at them, for civilization was to them almost as strange an experience as it was to those beasts and birds on Robinson Crusoe's island. Joe was already quite proficient with the shot-gun, and he often handed the lines to Rob, and stopping the team, got out and walked ahead of the wagons to stalk a flock of the beautiful game, which had been frightened away from their feeding-ground by the rattle of the teams. For a long time grouse was a part of every meal until the party became really tired of them. Mrs. Thompson was a famous cook, and they were served up in a variety of ways, but the favorite style of all the family was to have them broiled before the camp-fire on peeled willow twigs. Rob always regarded it as part of his duty to procure these twigs, as he was the handiest with a jack-knife or hatchet.

The weeks passed pleasantly for the children, but the old folks were becoming very anxious to settle somewhere, for the winter, as they thought, would soon be coming on. They did not know then that that season in Kansas is usually short, and that the three or four months preceding it is the most delightful time of the whole year. So after travelling nearly two months on the

broad trail to the mountains, examining a piece
of land here and another there, they camped
early one afternoon on the bank of Oxhide Creek,
in what is now Ellsworth County, and so delighted
were they all with the charming spot, that they
made up their minds to seek no further.

Their "claim," as the possession of the public
land is called, included a beautiful bend of the
little stream which flowed through the one hundred and sixty acres to which they were entitled
by being the first to settle on it. They discovered in the very centre of a group of elms and
cottonwoods a large spring of deliciously cool
water, and the trees which hid it from view were
more than a century old. The magnificent pool
for untold ages had evidently been a favorite
resort of the antelope and buffalo, if one could so
judge from the quantity of the bones of those
animals that were constantly ploughed up near by
when the ground was cultivated. No doubt that
the big prairie wolf and the cowardly little coyote
hidden in the long grass and underbrush surrounding the spring got many a kid and calf
whose incautious mothers had strayed from the
protection of the herd to quench their thirst.

The beautiful creek flowed at the base of a
range of low, rocky hills, while two miles northward ran a magnificent stretch of level prairie,
beyond which ran the Smoky Hill River.

To their ranche, as all homes in the far West
are called, the Thompsons gave the name of Errolstrath. It had no special significance; it was
so called merely because "Strath" in Scotch
means a valley through which a stream meanders.
It comported perfectly with the situation of the
place, and "Errol" was added as a prefix for
euphony's sake. In this picturesque little valley
Mr. Thompson, with the assistance of his boys,
began at once the construction of a rude but
comfortable cabin, fashioned partly out of logs
and partly of stone. The house outside gave no
hint of the excellence of its interior, or the cosy
rooms which a refined taste and culture had felt
to be as necessary on the remote frontier as in the
thickly settled East. The largest division of the
house was an apartment which served as the family sitting-room. In one corner of this, they built
diagonally across it, after the Mexican style, an
old-fashioned fireplace, patterned like one in the
ancestral homestead in Vermont. Up its cavern-

ous throat you could see the sky, and in the summer, when the full moon was at the zenith, a flood of bright light would pour down on the broad hearth. In the winter evenings the family gathered around the great blazing logs, whose yellow flames roared like a tornado as they shot up the chimney. The mother sewed, the girls were engaged with their studies, and the boys either listened to their father as he told of some experience in his own youthful days, played chess, or were busied with some other intellectual amusement.

This large room was also furnished with a small but well-selected library. It was a source of much pleasure to the family, as the country was not settled up very rapidly, and the members were thrown entirely upon their own resources for amusements. The following spring and summer many newcomers arrived and took up the choicest lands in the vicinity, until there were several families within varying distances of Errolstrath. Some were only three miles away, others twelve, but in that region then, all were considered neighbors, no matter how far away.

The children had lots of fun, for the rare sport

differed entirely from that which their former home in the old East had furnished. The dense timber which grew by the water of the Oxhide like a fringe, was the home of the lynx, erroneously called the wild cat, squirrels, badgers, and coons. The wolf and the little coyote had their dens in the great ledges of rock that were piled up on the hilly sides of the valley. The great prairie was often black with vast herds of buffalo, or bison, which roamed over its velvety area at certain seasons. The timid antelope, too, graceful as a flower, and gifted with a wonderful curiosity, could be seen for many years after the Thompsons had settled on the creek. They moved in great flocks, frequently numbering a thousand or more, but now, like their immense shaggy congener, the buffalo, through the wantonness of man, they have been almost annihilated.

Joe Thompson, the eldest child, about fourteen, was a rare boy, strongly built, and possessed of a mind that was equal to his well-developed body. He was a born leader, and became one of the most prominent men on the frontier when the troublous times came with the savages, some

years after the family had settled on Oxhide
Creek. Robert, the second son, was a bright,
active, muscular fellow, two years younger than
Joe, but he lacked that self-reliance, energy,
and coolness in the presence of danger which
so strikingly characterized Joe. Gertrude and
Kate were respectively ten and seven years old,
and were carefully instructed by their estimable
mother in all that should be known by a woman
whose life was destined, perhaps, to the isolation
and hardships of the frontier. They were both
taught to cook a dinner, ride horseback, handle
a pistol if necessary, or entertain gracefully in
the parlor. To employ a metaphor, theirs was
a versatility which "could pick up a needle or
rive an oak!" In some of her characteristics
Gertrude resembled her brother Joe; she was
braver and cooler under trying circumstances
than Kate, who was more like Rob. Both were
rare specimens of noble girlhood, and their life
on the ranche, as will be seen, was full of adventure and thrilling experiences.

It may seem strange that a stream should be
called Oxhide, but, like the nomenclature of the
Indians, the name of every locality out on the

great plains is based upon some incident connected with the scene or the individual. As
this is a true story, it will not be amiss to tell
here why the odd-sounding name was given to
the creek on which the Thompsons had settled.
Some years before the country was sought after
by emigrants, the only travellers through it were
the old-time trappers, who caught the various
fur-bearing animals on the margins of its waters,
and the miner destined for far-off Pike's Peak
or California. A party camping there one day,
on their way to the Pacific coast, discovered a
yoke of oxen, or rather their desiccated hides
and skeletons, fastened by their chains to a tree,
where they had literally starved to death. It
was supposed that they had belonged to some
travellers like themselves, on their way to the
mines, who had been surprised and murdered
by the Indians. The savages must have run
off the moment they had finished their bloody
work, without ever looking for or finding the
poor animals. Thus it was that the stream was
given the name of Oxhide, which it bears to
this day.

CHAPTER II

IT was quite late in the season, towards the end of October, when the stone and log cabin was completed and ready for occupancy. The family had meanwhile lived in their big tent which they had brought with them from the Missouri River. They had carried in their wagons bedding and blankets, a table and several chairs, enough to suffice until the arrival of their other goods, which had been stored at Leavenworth while they were hunting for a location. At the end of two months after their settlement on the Oxhide, a freight caravan arrived with their things, much of it the old-fashioned furniture from the homestead in Vermont. This caravan was en route to Fort Union, New Mexico, the trail to which military post ran along the bank of the Smoky Hill River, not more than two miles from the ranche.

Joe and Rob were constantly busy helping their father to make matters snug for the winter, building a corral for the cows, a stone stable for the horses, and a chicken house for the fowls, of which they had more than a hundred, Plymouth rocks and white leghorns, the best layers in the world. Up to that time they had not had as much time for sport as they wished for. They had been kept too busy, until long after the cold weather set in, when all the streams were frozen over and the woods were bare and brown.

A near neighbor who had taken a fancy to the bright lads when they first arrived in the country, had given them two fine greyhounds, which they named Bluey and Brutus; the former on account of his color, and the other because they had recently been interested in Shakespeare's play of "Julius Cæsar," which their father had read to them. With these magnificent animals they had lots of fun during the long months of the winter, hunting jack-rabbits, digging coyotes out of their holes in the ledge above the banks of the creek, or fighting lynxes and coons in the timber.

One bright day they were out among the hills with their hounds, which had run far in advance of their young masters, when suddenly the boys' ears were startled by a terrible commotion in a wooded ravine about a hundred yards ahead of them. The dogs were barking furiously, sometimes howling in pain, and they could see the dust flying in great clouds. In a few moments all was still; the turmoil had ceased, a truce evidently having been patched up between the belligerents. The boys hurried on and presently came to a sheltered spot where the timber had been apparently blown down by a small tornado many years before; and there as they came up to it, in a triangle formed by the trunks of three fallen trees, a space about ten feet square, they saw the hounds holding a great lynx at bay! The cat was standing in the apex of the triangle, crowding her body as closely as she could against the timber so that the dogs were unable to attack her without getting a scratch from her sharp claws. Her hair was all bristling up with battle, and the dogs had evidently tried several times to drive her out of her almost impregnable position, but each attempt had ended in themselves being driven back discomfited. As soon as the hounds saw the boys, however, their courage rose, and Bluey, the oldest dog, at an encouraging " Sic 'em!" from Joe, made a sudden dash, caught the ferocious beast by the middle of the back and commenced to shake her with the awful rapidity for which he was noted, and in a few seconds she was dropped dead at Joe's feet.

Bluey first became famous as a shaker several months before his encounter with the lynx. One morning Rob got up very early for some reason, and went into the chicken house, and as soon as he entered it he saw a skunk half hidden under one of the beams of the floor. He did not dare to call Bluey, who was sleeping on a pile of hay a few feet away, for fear the animal would take the alarm and run off. So he quietly went to where the dog was, and lifting him bodily in his arms carried him to the chicken house and held his nose down to the ground so that he could see or smell the skunk. In an instant that skunk was caught up by the neck and the life shaken out of him before he could have possibly realized what was the matter with him.

"By jolly!" said Rob, a favorite ejaculation with him when he was excited, as he saw the cat lying perfectly still where Bluey had dropped him. "I say, Joe, what a set of teeth and a strong neck old Bluey must have to shake anything as he does! Why, if he could take up a man in his jaws, the fellow would stand no more chance of his life than that lynx!"

"The hound," replied Joe, "has a strong jaw and a powerful neck; but he lacks the intelligence of some other breeds. His brain is not nearly as large as that of a Newfoundland, a setter, pointer, or even a poodle. Hounds like Bluey and Brutus run by sight alone; they have no nose, and the moment they cannot see their game they are lost. You have often noticed that, Rob, when a rabbit gets away from them in the long grass or in the corn stalks. They will jump up and down, completely bewildered until they catch sight of the animal again. Now, with the other breed of hounds, they hunt by scent; the moment they get wind of anything

c

they run with their noses close to the ground
and commence to howl. The greyhound, on the
contrary, makes no noise at all."

Joe skinned the lynx, assisted by Rob, and
after throwing the carcass in the ravine where
the battle had been fought, slowly walked back
to the ranche, followed by the dogs, that kept
close to their heels, tired and sore from the
struggle just ended.

"Let us give the hide to Gert after we tan it,
to put at the side of her bed; you know she is
fond of such things," said Rob.

"All right," replied Joe. "We'll do it, and
if we have good luck in getting other animals,
we'll just fill her room with skins. Won't that
be jolly?"

Mr. Thompson had but two teams of horses
on the ranche, and they could not often be spared
from work, for the mere amusement of the boys.
It was a constant source of regret to them that
they did not have ponies of their own. On their
way home the oft-repeated subject came up again.
Both Joe and Rob felt keenly that they were
obliged to go where they were sent, or desired
to go themselves, on foot. How to obtain the

coveted little creatures was a source of continual worry to them.

"I do wish that we had ponies," began Rob for the hundredth time, "so that we could go anywhere in a hurry; don't you, Joe?"

"Father would buy them for us if he felt that he could afford it; and he means to as soon as he can see his way clear. I heard him tell mother so, several times when she wished that we had 'em," replied Joe. "Maybe," continued he, "some band of friendly Indians will come along after a while; it's nearly time for the Pawnees to start out on their annual buffalo hunt. When they come up here, we may be able to trade 'em out of a real nice pair. They are always eager for a 'swap'; so old man Tucker told me the other day, and he is an old Indian trader and fighter. He has lived on the plains and in the mountains for more than forty years; so he knows what he is talking about."

"Golly! couldn't we have lots of fun," he continued, "with old Bluey and Brutus, after jack-rabbits and wolves, if we only had something to ride?"

"Couldn't we, though!" answered Rob. "I tell

you, Joe, it's awful hard work to climb over these hills on foot; we can't begin to keep up with the dogs; can't get anywhere in sight of 'em. You know that, and I just bet that we lose lots of game; don't you?"

"Oh! I know it," said Joe; "for the hounds become discouraged when they find themselves so far away from us. Often, when I'm out alone with them, Brutus will come back to hunt me instead of hunting rabbits. Sometimes I can't get him to go on after Bluey; he, the old rascal is more cunning; he gets many a rabbit we never see, and eats it. That is what makes him so much fatter than Brutus, though he does twice as much running. Did you ever think of that, Rob?"

That night when the tired boys went to bed, they little dreamed that they were to have something to ride sooner than their fondest hopes had flattered them, and from an entirely different source than the Indians.

Before the sun's broad disc rose above the Harker Hills next morning, although its rays had already crimsoned the rocky crests of the buttes which bounded the little valley of the

Oxhide on the west, Rob had risen without disturbing his brother. He was always an early riser; he loved the calm, beautiful hours that usher in the day, and was the first one of all the family out of bed on the ranche.

He took the tin wash basin from its hook outside of the kitchen door, and started for the spring, only a few yards away, to wash himself. Just as he arrived there, chancing to look towards the hills, he saw that the whole country, upland and bottom alike, was black with buffaloes. In his excitement, he threw down the basin, and ran back to the house as fast as his legs could carry him. He rushed into his father's room, and unceremoniously seizing him by the shoulder, waking him from a sound slumber, shook him, and shouted as loud as he was able : —

"Father, get up! Father, get up! the whole country is alive with buffaloes, and the nearest one is not a quarter of a mile away. Quick! father."

Mr. Thompson roused himself, and instantly got out of bed and dressed himself quicker than he had ever done since he had lived on the ranche. He threw on only clothes enough to cover him, for he had already caught some of his boy's enthusiasm.

He told Rob to go to the closet, bring him a dozen bullets and his powder-flask, while he commenced to wipe out the barrels of his two old-fashioned rifles and the Spencer carbine, that always hung on a set of elk antlers fastened to the wall of his bed-chamber.

As Rob had declared, the whole region was literally dark with a mighty multitude of the great shaggy monsters, grazing quietly toward the east. There were thousands in sight, and for just such a chance Mr. Thompson had been anxiously waiting to get a supply of meat for the family.

Of course, every member of the household got up as soon as Rob had ended his noisy announce-ment. Hurriedly dressing, they rushed out un-der a group of trees that grew near the door, and watched Mr. Thompson crawling cautiously round the rocks as he drew nearer and nearer to the yet unconscious herd.

In a few moments he was lost to sight, and almost immediately they saw the herd raise their heads simultaneously. The family then knew that Mr. Thompson had been discovered by the

wary animals, for the alarmed buffaloes began
their characteristic quick, short gallop, and the
boys were fearful that their father had not gotten
within range and that there would be no meat for
breakfast. But at the instant they were expecting to be disappointed, the loud crack of a rifle
echoed through the valley once, twice, then a
short silence ; three, four times.

As the sound of the discharges died away,
they saw their father climb to the summit of the
divide, in full view of all, and wave his hat.
Then they knew he had been successful, and
eagerly watched him as he came slowly down the
declivity toward them.

When he had come within hailing distance he
cried out that he had killed four fat cows ; one
for each shot. Then the boys and girls took off
their hats, and, vigorously waving them, gave
three hearty cheers.

Just beyond the cabin and corral, which latter
was surrounded by a stone wall nearly five feet
high, was a single hill whose summit was round,
and to which had been given the name of Haystack Mound, because at a distance it exactly
resembled a haystack. When the buffaloes had

started to run eastwardly, this mound cut off some of the animals of the herd, about three hundred in all, the majority going south of it, the smaller number north, which brought them near the house. Seeing the family standing there, they suddenly turned and rushed right over the corral; the gate was open, and a few dashed through it, but the most of them leaped over the wall. The buffalo is not easily stopped by any ordinary obstacle when stampeded; he will go down a precipice, or up a steep hill; madly rushing on to his destruction, in order to get away from the common enemy, man.

Rob saw the buffaloes first as they were turned from their course by the mound, and when they began to rush over the wall of the corral and through its gate, he shouted to Joe: —

"Come, Joe, let's try to shut some of them in; maybe there are calves among them. If there are, we can keep 'em in, for the little ones can never mount that wall on the other side."

Instantly acting on the suggestion, both boys ran as fast as they could to the corral, and succeeded in closing the entrance just as the last of the herd was leaping over the far wall.

As Rob had surmised, four calves remained inside, too young to follow their mothers over the wall. Both he and Joe were nearly wild with excitement at their luck in having been able to shut the gate in time to corral the baby buffaloes. They were about to rush to the house to tell the rest of the family of their wonderful capture, when Joe chanced to look into the door of the rude shed that was used to shelter the stock in stormy weather, and saw jammed against the farther wall two animals that were too small to be full-grown buffaloes, and too large for calves. It was so dark in the corner where they were that he could not make out at first what kind of animals they had caught. He called Rob, who crawled nearer to where the beasts stood huddled against each other, trembling with fear at their strange quarters.

In another moment, as soon as Rob's eyes became used to the dim light, he came bounding out with the speed of a Comanche Indian on the war-path, and catching Joe by the shoulders was just able to gasp: —

" By jolly, Joe, they're real ponies!"

They were so astonished for a few seconds

that they stood paralyzed before they ventured in the shed to take a good look at the little animals. They boldly went in, and the moment the ponies saw the boys they made a break for the outside and vainly attempted to dash over the wall. Their frantic efforts, however, were of no avail; they could not make it: they were regular prisoners, and Rob and Joe were almost out of their senses with delight.

After their excitement had somewhat subsided they went to the house and brought out all the rest of the family to see the cunning little animals. They lost all their interest in the buffalo calves now that their brightest dreams of owning ponies of their own were realized.

The diminutive beasts which the boys had so successfully corralled were sorry-looking animals enough. They were so dirty, thin, angular, and their coats so rough, so filled with sand-burrs and bull-nettles, that it was hard to determine what color they were. All the family made a guess at it. Kate said she thought they were mouse-color, while Gertrude believed they were gray. Joe thought they were brown, and Rob white. Mr. Thompson, however, who knew more about horses than his boys, told them they were bays, but it would take a few days of currying and brushing up to determine which of the family had guessed correctly. There was evidently lots of life in them, for they cavorted around the big corral, prancing like thoroughbreds.

That afternoon, when they had taken care of the buffaloes which Mr. Thompson shot, and had stretched their robes on the corral wall to cure, the ponies were roped by Mr. Thompson, who could handle a lariat with some degree of skill, and halters were put on them. They were nearly of a size, and both of the same color, so they could hardly be distinguished from each other, but on a closer examination it was discovered that one of them had a white spot on his breast. This was the only apparent difference between them, so the boys drew lots to see which should have the one with the white breast. Their father selected two straws, one shorter than the other, and holding them partly concealed so that only their ends showed, told Rob to draw first. He got the longer straw, and so became the owner of the pony with the spot of white on his breast.

In less than two weeks, through kindness and good care, they were changed into clean, sleek, beautiful bays, just as Mr. Thompson had said they would be.   In a month the boys could ride them anywhere, and the acme of their happiness was reached.

The animals had strayed from some band of wild horses and had drifted along with the herd of buffaloes, as was not infrequently the case in the early days on the great plains.

CHAPTER III

THE winter, contrary to their expectations, was
not a severe one. The family had been used to
the long, dreary, cold months of a New England
winter, and were agreeably surprised when April
arrived with its sunny skies, delicious breezes,
and wild flowers covering the prairies.

One morning, when his father was just starting for the little village of Ellsworth, six miles
distant, for a load of lumber, Rob asked him to
buy some hooks and lines.

"Father," said he, "Oxhide Creek is just full
of bull-pouts, perch, cat and buffalo fish. Joe
and I want to go fishing to-day, if you return in
time."

Mr. Thompson told the boys that he would
not forget them, and as he drove off, they took
their spades to dig in the garden as their father
had directed them to do while he was away.

Both Joe and Rob worked very industriously,
anxious to make the time slip away until their
father's return, when, if he was satisfied with
what they had done, they knew he would let
them go fishing.

Just before twelve o'clock Mr. Thompson came
back.   The boys had worked for more than
three hours, but it seemed only one to them, so
quickly does time glide along when we are engaged in some healthful labor.

When Mr. Thompson saw how faithfully his
boys had worked, he told them, as he handed to
each a line and some hooks, they might have the
afternoon to themselves and go fishing if they
wished to, but must wait until they had taken
the lumber off the wagon and eaten their dinner.

The boys were all excitement at the idea of
going fishing.   When they sat down to dinner
they hurried through it, asked to be excused, and
went out and unloaded the lumber before their
father had done eating.

When they returned to the house and told their father they had unloaded the boards and run the wagon under the shed, he said they might go, but were to be sure to return in time to do the chores.

They took a spade from the tool-shed and an old tomato can their mother had given them, and started for the creek, where in the soft, black soil of its banks they dug for white grubs for bait. They were not very successful, however. They turned over almost as much soil as they had dug in the garden that morning, but found only three or four worms; not enough to take out on their excursion. They were disgusted for a few moments, fearing that they would have to give up their fishing, so stood staring at each other, their faces filled with disappointment.

At last an idea struck Rob. He said:—

" I'll tell you what we'll do, Joe. I read in one of father's books the other day about the Indians out in Oregon catching trout with crayfish. It said that the savages commence to fish far up at the head of the stream, lifting, as they walk down, the flat stones under which the little animals hide themselves. They look like small lobsters,

only they are gray instead of green. Then they
break them open and use the white meat for bait.
The book said they catch more trout in an hour
than a white man will in a week with all his flies,
bugs, and fancy rigging."

" Let's try 'em for luck," answered Joe. " I don't
know whether there are any crayfish in the Oxhide, but we can go and find out; and if there
are, I guess cat and perch will bite at 'em as
well as trout."

" All right," said Rob, the look of disappointment instantly vanishing from his face as he
listened to his brother's suggestion. " But I
tell you, Joe," continued he, " we've got to have
poles. You go up to that bunch of willows
yonder," pointing with the old can he held in
his hand, to the bunch of willows growing as
thick as rushes on a little island in the creek,
about an eighth of a mile from where he stood;
"and here, Joe, take my line and hooks, too.
Fix yours and mine all ready for us, while I go
and hunt for the crayfish. I know where they
are; I saw a whole lot crawling in the water
near the house the other day."

The two brothers then separated, — Joe, jack-knife in hand, going toward the willows, and Rob to the creek with the tomato can.

As soon as Rob arrived at the bank of the stream, he took off his boots and stockings, rolled his trousers above his knees, tied the can around his neck with a string, and waded in. The creek was not at all deep, and the water as clear as crystal. He could see shoals of perch dart ahead of him, and many bull-pouts rush under the shadow of the bank as he waded toward the island of willows. In the bed of the creek were hundreds of flat rocks; some that he could easily lift, others so large that he could not budge them.

The first stone he turned over had three of the coveted crayfish hidden under its slimy bottom, and excited at his luck, he quickly caught them. So many were there as he lifted stone after stone, that he soon filled the tomato can, and by that time he had arrived at the willows. Joe was anxiously waiting for him with two handsome rods, at least ten feet long, the lines already attached and the hooks nicely fastened to their ends.

"Golly! Rob, you must have had awful good

D

luck," said Joe, as he looked at the can full of struggling crayfish.

" Pshaw!" answered Rob. " Why, Joe, I could have got a bushel of 'em ; the Oxhide was just swimming with 'em."

" Let's go to that little lake that was so nice where we went swimming last autumn," suggested Joe. " I know there are lots of cats in there; big ones, too."

" All right, Joe," said Rob, as he commenced to put on his stockings. When he had got his boots on, the two boys walked briskly toward the so-called lake, which was a mere widening of the creek, forming quite a large sheet of water, where they arrived in about seven minutes. It was a very delightful spot. The whole surface of the water was shaded by the gigantic limbs of great elms a hundred years old, growing on its margin, and all around the edge was a heavy mat of buffalo grass, soft as a carpet.

It required only a dozen seconds or so for the boys to unwind their lines, bait the hooks, seat themselves on the cushioned sod, and cast the shining white meat in the water.

There they anxiously waited for results, as the catfish is not game like the trout, but is slow and deliberate in all its movements. The trout rushes at anything that touches the surface of the water, but the catfish carefully investigates whatever comes within reach of its great jaws, before it opens its ugly mouth to take it in.

In a few minutes, Rob felt a tremendous tugging at his line, and in another instant he skilfully landed a large channel cat on the grass at his feet.

" Look, Joe, look! see what a big one I've caught," said Rob, as he dexterously extracted the hook from the creature's great mouth, and then held the fish at arm's length so that his brother could have a good look at it.

Rob's catch weighed at least four pounds, and no wonder he was delighted at such success, as it showed considerable skill to land a fish of that size.

Joe had not yet had a nibble, and a shade of disappointment began to creep over his face when suddenly, just as he was about to go over to examine his brother's catch more closely, he

was nearly jerked off his feet by a tremendous
pull at his own line. He recovered himself immediately, and by dint of a hard struggle, hauled
in a cat that was almost as big again as that
which Rob had caught.

It was Joe's turn to yell now; he held up the
big fish as high as he could, — its tail touched
the ground even then, — and sung out: —

"I say, Rob, just look at this, will you?
Yours is only a minnow alongside of mine.
When you go fishing, why don't you catch
something like this?"

Unfortunately, at the instant he was so wild
with excitement, he stood on the very edge
of the bank, and so absorbed was he in the
contemplation of the great fish, that his foot
slipped and both he and the cat were thrown
into the water at the same moment. The cat
made a terrible lunge forward when it found
itself once more in its native element, and before
you could say "Jack Robinson," was out of sight.

If ever disgust was to be seen on a boy's face,
that face was Joe Thompson's; he only glanced
at the water, did not say a word; his feelings
were too sad for utterance.

Rob looked over at his brother and sarcastically said, as he held up his cat and stroked it: —

"I say, Joe, who's got the biggest fish now?"

In an instant he saw that he had touched Joe in a tender spot; he was a very sensitive boy, so Rob quickly added: "Well, never mind, Joe. You remember what mother often says to us, 'There is as good a fish in the sea as was ever caught,' and I'll bet there's just as big cats in here as the one you lost. Try again, Joe, but stand away from the edge of the water with the next one you haul out."

Joe, thus encouraged and comforted, sat down again in his old place, threw his line to try once more, and in the excitement soon forgot his misfortune.

In less than three hours the boys caught more than a dozen apiece, none so large, however, as that which escaped from Joe. It was now nearly six o'clock, the sun was low in the heavens, and as they had as many fish as they could conveniently carry, they decided to go home. Arriving there in a short time, they at once went to work at their chores. Their customary evening's task was to drive the cows into the corral, feed the horses and their own ponies, and bring water from the spring for their mother, so that it should be handy when she rose in the morning.

While Joe and Rob were at their work, their father cleaned some of the fish, which their mother then cooked for supper, and they certainly tasted to the young anglers better than ever did fish before. While at the table they related every little incident that had befallen them on this their first angling expedition in the new country.

After that very successful excursion the brothers sometimes spent whole mornings or portions of the afternoons at some place on the creek or river, when the work on the ranche was not pushing, and so expert did they become with hook and line, that the family was never at a loss for a supply of fish during the proper seasons.

Joe was a close observer of nature, and he very quickly learned the habits of all the animals, birds, and fish that were common to the region where he lived. Being the eldest son, too, he was intrusted with a small but excellent rifle and a shot-gun which his father bought one morning in the village, on the fifteenth anniversary of his birthday. He would get up very early in the morning and with his pony and the hounds have many a lively chase after the little cotton-tail rabbit or the larger "jack," improperly so called, for it is really the hare. The rabbit burrows in the ground, while the jack-rabbit does not, but makes his nest on the top, in a bunch of grass, or in the holes in the rocky ledges of the bluffs that fringe nearly every stream on the great plains. Out on the open prairies the grouse congregated in large flocks at certain seasons, and in every covert in the woods the quail could be found. Joe had really handled a gun long before he left Vermont, but the superior chance for practice out on the ranche soon made him a magnificent shot; consequently the table at the ranche was never without game if the family desired it.

Beside the smaller game I have mentioned, there were immense herds of buffalo and ante-lope, and in some places in the deep woods was the only long-tailed specimen of the genus felis

on the continent, — the cougar, or panther. All
the wildcats, so called, are lynxes, with short tails.
With one of the first mentioned Joe once had a
severe tussle, which nearly proved disastrous to
him. It happened in this way.

One afternoon in November shortly after the
cabin was finished and the family had moved in,
he was out on the range with his father's horse,
the Spencer carbine, and about twenty rounds of
ammunition. Even at that early stage of his life
at Errolstrath he was always careful never to ride
far away from home, without taking a gun with
him; for he was always sure to see something in
the shape of game worth killing for the table;
and as its main support in that particular very
soon depended on his prowess as a hunter, he
was always on the lookout.

Joe had ridden a long way from the cabin.
He had really forgotten how far away he was and
was becoming very thirsty, for the day had been
warm, so he commenced to hunt for water.

He was riding along the bank of the Smoky
Hill in the thickest of the timber which grows
on its banks, and by certain signs he had
studied since he had lived on the ranche, knew

that he was near some springs, though he had never been in that vicinity before.

He got off his horse, slipped the loop of the bridle-rein over his left arm, slung the carbine across his right shoulder, and cautiously walked on. There was, of course, no trail or path at the base of the bluffs along which he was travelling, so he stopped at the mouth of every ravine he came to, hoping to find a pool of water, or to discover some hidden spring whose source was high up among the great rocks that towered above his head.

Presently he arrived at a depression in the earth in the bottom of a gully, evidently made by the claws of some animal, for beside those marks were the imprint of foot-tracks. Joe intuitively guessed they were those of a panther, as he had been told by the old trapper, Tucker, that that animal knows by instinct when the water is near the surface, and scratches with his claws until he reaches it. Joe knew, too, that the panther was not a very large one; his footprints were too small; so he did not feel at all alarmed at their sight. On the contrary, boy-like, he was delighted at the idea of a possible tussle with one of the dreadful creatures, and he thought that if he could succeed in killing it he would add another feather to his cap by taking its hide home.

Joe felt himself equal to a possible struggle. He knew that he was fully armed, and at once examined his carbine, took out the knife which he always carried in his belt for skinning, and finding everything in perfect order, he was really anxious to find the animal that had been digging for water only a little while before his arrival at the spot.

A few rods further on, in the same ravine, he saw a little pool of water, evidently clear and cool, and after looking cautiously all around him, dipped the rim of his hat into the pool before him and indulged in a long drink of the delicious fluid. Then after having satisfied his thirst, he stood still for a few moments undecided as to what course he should pursue.

He concluded that if he was to remain and fight the panther if the animal made his appearance, it would be best to tie his horse to a sapling a short distance from the pool. After doing this he placed a fresh cartridge in his carbine and walked slowly on, following the beast's tracks, which had grown plainly visible a few paces from the edge of the water, and which soon led him into a rocky cañon.

Joe came in sight of the panther much sooner than he expected. As he was turning the sharp projecting corner of a mass of rocks which formed the walls of a ravine, there was the panther sitting on a shelf of sandstone, not forty feet away from him. He was busy licking his paws cat-fashion, his ears cocked as if listening, and his small green eyes turned toward the intruder, but evidently not much concerned at the sight of his greatest enemy, man.

Joe was rather taken aback at first, but as the brute was only a little over half-grown, and appeared so indifferent to his presence, he uncocked his carbine, which he had a moment before hastily cocked, and both boy and panther stood quietly gazing at each other for ten seconds before either made any demonstration.

Presently the panther rose and turned sideways toward Joe, and edging up toward the top of the ledge, gave vent to a low growl, and showed a beautiful set of long, sharp teeth, evidently

intending to let Joe know that he wasn't afraid of
him.   This movement on the part of the panther
somewhat excited Joe, and cocking his carbine
again, he deliberately took aim at the place where
the heart of the beast should be, as the animal
had now turned its left side toward the young
hunter.   Quick as a flash Joe pulled the trigger,
but the ball glancing upward, only grazed the end
of the beast's shoulder-blade and shattered it, the
panther at the same instant tumbling over on its
side.   This made Joe yell with delight, for he
thought he had killed it at the first shot.

The panther lay on the ground only for about
ten seconds when the aspect of affairs for Joe was
suddenly changed.   The brute staggered to its
feet, and, maddened with rage and pain, made for
the boy.   Although the beast was evidently very
lame from the effect of the shot, Joe saw to his
amazement that he was far from dead, and for a
moment his usual presence of mind forsook him,
and he made a bolt for his horse, feeling that the
dreadful animal was close to him.

In his fright he dropped his carbine, but in
another moment was on his horse, who, on being
so unceremoniously mounted, and seeing the

"With one vigorous thrust of his knife he struck the animal's heart."

panther, gave a wild snort and a desperate kick
which sent Joe heels over head to the ground,
and then dashed down the trail for home!

Joe was now all alone, on foot, and with
nothing but his knife to defend himself from
the attack of the panther, who was almost
upon him as he got up from the ground after
having been so hurriedly tossed from his saddle. Although the panther was lame and
bleeding profusely, he waddled along as best
he could toward Joe, his mouth wide open and
his great jaws covered with froth in his rage.
Joe was somewhat bruised by his fall, and seeing very quickly that he could not escape a
tussle with the beast, made up his mind that
he would fight him to the best of his ability.
There was no other chance, for the panther
was now upon him, trying to get at him so
that he could claw and bite at his leisure.
But Joe, who had now gained his normal coolness, turned deliberately, and facing the savage
brute, whose hot breath he could feel, with one
vigorous thrust of his knife he struck the animal's heart and fortunately killed him instantly.

In the close struggle the panther was so near

Joe, that in his death throes, having fallen right
on top of the boy, his sharp claws tore the
sleeve of his coat off and scratched a goodly
piece of flesh from his arms, as with one con-
vulsive shudder the ferocious animal had rolled
over dead.

There was never a more delighted boy than
Joe, despite his really painful wounds, and rising with some difficulty to his feet, he went
back for his carbine, and returned with it to
the dead panther. He picked up his knife
which had fallen on the ground when the
fatal thrust was given, deftly skinned him, suspended the beautiful hide to a limb of a cottonwood tree to keep the wolves from it, and
then turned away and followed his trail towards
the ranche. Of course, in a little while he began to grow stiff in his arms from the sever-
ity of his wounds, and not knowing exactly
how far he was from the cabin, he was disturbed, not so much for himself as at the
thought that when the riderless horse arrived
there it would alarm his parents.

Joe was correct in his conjectures. As the
horse dashed up to the stable without his

rider, both his father and mother were terribly frightened. They plucked up courage, however, and immediately saddling another horse, led back on his own trail the one Joe had ridden, and soon came up to where Joe was resting at the side of a large spring, and suffering considerably with the pain caused by his wounds.

They all arrived at the cabin by sundown, with the skin of the panther, Joe's father having gone back to the tree where the boy had hung it. That was a red-letter day in Joe's young life. He had to tell again and again how he happened to come on the panther and his awful fight with the enraged creature.

Joe soon recovered under the devoted nursing of his mother; his arm healed nicely, but a good-sized scar was left where the panther had dug its sharp claws into the flesh. The hide was smoke-tanned, and for many years afterward adorned the floor at the foot of his mother's bed.

CHAPTER IV

BOY AND GIRL LIFE AT ERROLSTRATH RANCHE — THEIR PETS —
THE GIRLS ENCOUNTER A BIG PRAIRIE WOLF — JOE TO THE
RESCUE — DEATH OF THE FEROCIOUS BEAST

As the months rolled on, the family, particularly the children, grew more and more delighted with their new home in the wilderness. The boys and girls had an abundance of leisure; for though their father exacted the most prompt obedience, he was not a hard task-master. He allowed his children every indulgence compatible with reason, and only certain portions of the day were devoted to work. They all studied under their father's personal supervision, for no schools had yet been established in the settlement.

For the boys, there were the cows to be driven to and from their pasture, morning and night, and it was their duty to milk them, too. Then the horses were to be fed, and in season they worked in the large garden, on which their father prided himself. The girls helped their mother in every household duty, and relieved her of many cares as she grew older. So the children of Errolstrath Ranche had a good time—a much better time than generally falls to the lot of those families in only moderate circumstances, as were the Thompsons.

Before they had resided on the ranche a year, the boys and girls had become possessed of a variety of pets. Gertrude had a coon; Kate, an antelope; Rob, a prairie dog; and Joe, an elk.

The antelope was caught when young by Joe, and the hounds, Bluey and Brutus, under the following circumstances: Although one of the most timid and swift of all the ruminants on the great plains, it is also one of the most inquisitive. Whenever it sees something with which it is not familiar, its curiosity overpowers its usual fear, and it will approach very near to the object that has excited its attention. Now Joe had learned from old Tucker, the trapper, just how the Indians act, when out hunting the antelope, to draw the herd within

E

range of their arrows. He said that sometimes
one or two of the savages would stand on
their heads and shake their legs in the air;
then again, they would hold up a blanket, no
matter what color, and wave it slowly, when the
herd, or at least a number from it, would gradually walk toward the Indians who were lying
flat on the ground, and thus become easy victims
to their swift, unerring arrows.

It was this knowledge of the antelope's prominent characteristic that enabled Joe to secure
one for his favorite sister. He was out very
early one morning when he noticed a large
herd with many kids among it, about half a
mile distant. He was well aware that his dogs,
swift as they were, would be no match for the
beautiful creatures in a trial of speed, so he
resolved to resort to the Indian method. Order-
ing his hounds to lie close, he tied his white
handkerchief round his head, and taking off
his overalls, he began to move his body slowly
backward and forward, at the same time vigorously waving the overalls in the air. In a few
moments, just as he expected they would, he
had the satisfaction of seeing first one, then

another, look up and gaze steadily at the strange
object. Presently, about half a dozen of the
does with their little ones by their sides, commenced to move cautiously towards him. When
they had approached sufficiently near, he started
the hounds after them, and after a short, lively
chase they caught a fine kid, which, of course,
could not keep up with its mother. They captured it without injury, for they had been trained
not to mouth their game. As there were a
dozen cows on the ranch, there was an abundance of milk, with which Kate used to feed her
little pet from a bottle. The pretty creature
throve rapidly, and soon became as affectionate
as a kitten, following its mistress everywhere like
a dog.

The big gray wolf, that ghoul of the great
plains, understands full well the inordinate curiosity of the antelope, and knowing that it is impossible for him to catch one of the fleet animals
by the employment of his legs alone, he effects
by cunning what he could never accomplish by
the best efforts of his endurance. The wicked
old fellow, when he discovers a bunch of ante-
lopes in the distance, rolls himself into a ball, like

a badger, and tumbles about on the grass until some of the deluded animals come near enough for him to spring on them.

Gertrude's coon was caught by both the boys, assisted by Bluey and Brutus. They dug him out of his nest under the roots of a huge elm tree near the cabin, one day in the early springtime, when the warm sun had just begun to thaw him after his winter's hibernation. He was "'cute" and mischievous as he could be, stealing anything on which he could get his tiny paws. Whenever Gertrude called him, — his name was Tom, — he would run to her as fast as he could, jump on her back, and sit on her shoulders for an hour at a time, when she was sewing or doing something which did not require her to move about. He lived on any scraps from the table, always rolling his food in his paws before he ate it.

The prairie dog, the property of Rob, was accidentally captured by Gertrude one morning when she and Kate were out gathering wild flowers. She actually stumbled on him as she stooped to pick a sensitive rose. The little creature had somehow become entangled in the convolutions of the vine, and thus became an easy prey. It fought like a tiger at first, and tried to bite with its sharp teeth everything that came near it. It was soon tamed, however, and became a regular nuisance at times, for it would run under your feet in spite of the many pinches it got by being stepped upon. It tripped up the boys and girls a dozen times a day, as it was allowed the freedom of the house and the dooryard. Gertrude gave it to Rob, who had often expressed a desire to own one, and had failed a hundred times, perhaps, to capture one by drowning it out of its hole.

The elk was given to Joe by old Tucker, and in a short time grew to be as big as a young mule. Joe broke him to harness, and used to drive him hitched to a little cart which his father, with the boy's help, improvised out of an odd pair of wheels and a dry-goods box. He was kept in the corral with the cows and horses, and became very tame, but sometimes attempted to use his sharp front hoofs too freely. He was forbidden the precincts of the dooryard and the house, for he came near cutting Kate in two once, all in play, but too rough a kind of affection for a repetition of it to be allowed.

The wild raspberries grew in great profusion near every ledge of rock in the vicinity of the ranche. About a mile and a half from the house, however, there was a specially favored spot for them, where the vines were more dense and the berries of large size and delicious flavor. In the second week of June, the second year of their residence on the creek, Rob, who had been up the valley herding the cows, reported that evening, upon his return, that the berries were ripe and that there were bushels of them.

The next morning, immediately after breakfast, Gertrude and Kate left the house with a tin bucket each, intending to go up to the ledge and gather raspberries. They were dressed lightly,— Kate in a white muslin skirt, and her sister in a lawn. As the nearest way to the place where the berries were to be found lay by a trail on the other side of the Oxhide the girls crossed it near the cabin, and as there was neither log bridge nor stepping-stones, they took off their shoes and stockings and waded it. After reaching the other side and putting on their shoes and stockings, they wandered slowly through a little flower-bedecked prairie, beyond the margin of

timber which fringed the creek, to make a short
cut to where the raspberries grew, for the Oxhide
made a sweeping curve to the northeast, nearly
in the shape of half a circle.

Both loving flowers, they gathered great
bunches of the sensitive roses, anemones, and
white daisies, growing everywhere in such profusion. This occupation consumed a great deal
of time, for they naturally loitered, charmed by
so much floral beauty around them. It was
fortunate they did, as the sequel will show, and
they did not arrive at the ledge of rocks until
nearly ten o'clock — more than two hours after
they had left home. It was intensely hot, and
after gathering their buckets full of the delicious
fruit, they sat down on a shelf of the ledge which
projected over the creek. They dabbled their
bare feet in the stream as it flowed in murmur-
ing rhythm over the rounded white pebbles, while
they ate their lunch of cake brought from the
ranche, and the red berries so sweet in the wild-
ness of their flavor.

Having satisfied their hunger, Kate said to
her sister: "Gert, we ought to fill up our
buckets again. If we go home empty-handed,

mother will think we have been making pigs of ourselves."

"There's time enough for that yet," replied Gertrude. "This cool water feels so delightful to my feet that I believe I could sit here and dabble in it until dark. Don't you think it's delicious, Kate?"

"Yes," answered Kate, "but I want to get home before dinner, because Joe said that he would go with me down to the village this evening. I am going to ride his pony, and he will ride Rob's."

"Well," said Gertrude, "if we must, we must. Mother loves raspberries so; they are her favorite fruit, you know; and if we did not take her a bucketful back with us, I should never forgive myself, though perhaps she would not say a word."

"Let us commence right now," imploringly said Kate. "I want to get back as soon as I can."

Both girls rose languidly to do as they proposed, but there did not seem to be much energy in their motions. Just as Gertrude had taken her pail from its place in the rocks, their ears were

greeted by a low growl, which seemed to come
directly from underneath the shelf on which they
had been sitting. They looked at each other,
and their faces blanched as another snarl and
a howl, nearer than before, came to their ears,
and both recognized the familiar sound they had
so often heard when lying in bed at night, as that
of a wolf. Those predatory brutes frequently
made their nightly rounds in the vicinity of the
corral, trying to get at the young calves, and
they might be heard in the timber, watching for
a chance to secure some of the fowls shut up in
their house of stone near the barn.

Gertrude, who was really very brave under
ordinary circumstances, immediately stood still,
and looking all around her, she suddenly met the
gaze of a large, gaunt she-wolf at whose side were
standing six little ones! Generally the wolf, like
nearly all other wild animals, will run instantly
at the sight of a human being; but the maternal
instinct is so wonderful that, when they have
young, they will die in defending their offspring
from any supposed danger. This instinct was
shown in this instance. The fierce animal had
crept out of her den at the sound of voices, and

believing that her cubs were in jeopardy, she made a frantic dash toward the now thoroughly frightened girls, who hastily scrambled to the summit of the ledge.

Fortunately for them, the wolf is a poor climber, but with a savage bound toward the base of the flat rock on which the girls had a moment before been sitting, she arrived at it the same instant they had succeeded in reaching an elevation of about twelve feet above the level of the water.

Just as Kate, who was not as collected as her sister, was being dragged up by Gertrude, the wolf made a desperate leap and snapped at her with his terrible teeth, but failed. It succeeded, however, in catching her skirt in its ponderous jaws, and tore it completely from her waist, and she, almost feeling the hot breath of the infuriated brute, uttered a loud scream and fell fainting in her sister's arms.

Less than three hundred yards above the ledge of rocks, in a beautiful piece of prairie, Joe was herding the cattle, and Kate's cry, so full of fear, fell piercingly on his ears. He was aware that his sisters were to go berrying that morning, and he also knew that the sound could only come from one of them. He was lying on the grass under the shade of a big elm with the bridle-rein of his pony in his hand. Grasping his rifle, which was at his side, in an instant he had mounted his animal, and digging his heels into its flanks, fairly flew down the creek to where his sisters were held at bay by the wolf. He arrived there in less than three minutes after he heard the scream of alarm, and saw the wolf still persisting in its vain efforts to reach the girls on the summit of the ledge. Gertrude was almost paralyzed with fear, and Kate lay at her feet in the swoon into which the action of the wolf had thrown her.

The enraged beast was too much occupied with the girls to notice that its would-be victims had assistance so near at hand, and Joe, as Gertrude saw her brother's approach, put his finger to his lips, indicating that she must remain perfectly silent. He dismounted in a second, and putting the loop of the reins over his left arm, dropped on one knee, and taking careful aim, sent a ball crashing right through the brain of the wolf, which instantly fell dead in its tracks.

Joe then rushed down to the creek and filled his hat with water. He then climbed hurriedly up to the rocky steep again and threw the water into Kate's face as she still lay prone on the ledge at her sister's feet. Kate soon revived, and after staring around her for a few seconds in a dazed way, she smiled and said: —

"Oh, Joe, you have saved us!" and rising to her feet, forgetful of her wet face, she kissed him half a dozen times.

While his sisters were adjusting their dresses and recovering from their terrible fright, Joe killed the young wolves with the butt of his rifle, and then taking his knife from his belt commenced to skin the old one. It did not require much time to perform the operation, for he had long since become an adept at such work. He then threw the beautiful hide over the withers of his pony, and walked home with his sisters.

Arriving at the cabin, the girls had much to tell about their wonderful experience and lucky escape from the jaws of the wolf, which would certainly have torn them to pieces if it had not been for Joe's timely arrival.

The hide, which was an immense one, was first tacked to the side of the stable, and when dried, Joe smoke-tanned it until it was as soft as a piece of silk. He gave it to Kate as a memento of her awful experience with its former owner. She used it as a rug at the side of her bed, and often said that for a long time whenever she stepped on it, the scene in which it played such an important part was brought vividly to her mind.

CHAPTER V

THE Pawnees and Kaws, tribes of Indians long at peace with the whites, and whose reservations were in the eastern part of the state, frequently made incursions into the buffalo region two hundred miles from their home in the valley of the Neosho, on their annual hunt for their winter's supply of meat. The valley of the Oxhide was one of their favorite camping-grounds, and from thence they radiated in bands to the plains, where the vast herds of the great shaggy animals grazed in the autumn months, on their curious elliptical march from the Yellowstone to the southern border of Texas.

Every autumn these Indians camped in the timber only about a mile from Errolstrath ranche, and it was very natural that the boys, especially

Joe, should often visit their temporary village, as
it was decidedly a new sensation for them. The
tepees, or lodges, built in a conical shape out of
long poles covered with well-tanned buffalo hides,
were a never-ending curiosity to Joe. The chief
of the band, Yellow Calf, an old man nearly
eighty years of age, took a great fancy to Joe
from the moment he first saw him. As soon as
he became acquainted with his character he called
him "White Panther," after the strange nomenclature of the North American savage. The Indians noticed immediately that Joe was different
from the majority of white children they had met,
and his quickness of motion was the reason they
named him as they did. His readiness in acquir-
ing their language, which he almost mastered in
a few months, astonished them. Then Joe was
always kind and gentle to the band, often bring-
ing food from his mother's table when she could
give it to him, especially bread or biscuit, of which
old Yellow Calf was inordinately fond. At the
suggestion of the chief, the closest warriors of his
council took great delight in showing their new
boy friend the use of the bow and arrow. They
taught him how to prepare the skins of animals

he shot ; how to make the robe of the buffalo as
soft as a doeskin, and they taught him how to
trap beaver, otter, and muskrat, in which valuable
fur-bearing animals all the streams abounded.
Yellow Calf would sit for hours talking with Joe,
learning from him all about the strange inven-
tions of the white man, and their uses. He in
turn taught the boy the mysteries of the beautiful sign language, so wonderful in its symbolism;
and the manner of trailing, so that in a few
months he was as well versed in the methods of
following an enemy on the warpath as the savages themselves.

The Indians frequently took Joe with them far
up the Arkansas valley on their grand hunts
after the buffalo. His parents readily gave their
consent to his going with his red friends, though
he was sometimes absent from home for more
than a week. For three seasons the same band
of Pawnees had their village on the creek, remaining there during the months of September
and October of each year. All that time Joe
continued his intimacy with them, and became
more perfect in his knowledge of their savage
methods. He could follow the blindest trail by

day or night, and the signs of the various hostile
tribes were as familiar to him as the alphabet.

He had been carefully trained to all this
knowledge by the Pawnees, who were the hereditary enemies of the Cheyennes who still claimed
sovereignty over the great plains. Once, in fact,
when he had been out for a fortnight with his
Indian friends on a buffalo hunt, the party was
suddenly met by a band of Cheyennes, and, of
course, a battle ensued to which Joe was a witness. After the fight that night, when the band
camped on the Walnut, he saw the dances of
the victorious Pawnees and learned a great deal
about savage warfare.

Shortly after the advent of the Pawnees on the
Oxhide, and when Joe had established his friendly
relations with them, although he could shoot
fairly well previously, he now began to take a
special delight in hunting. Every moment he
could get to himself, he was off in the timber or
out on the prairie with his rifle or shot-gun.
He never carried these, however, unless he
hunted alone, as on many occasions he was accompanied by one or two of the Pawnee boys
about his own age whom the band had brought

F

with them; young bucks, not yet old enough to have reached the dignity of warriors. They had to do the work generally assigned to the women, for no squaws were with the band. It is beneath a warrior to do anything but hunt, eat, smoke, and go to war; for idleness is the predominant characteristic of the men of every savage race, and the Pawnees were no exception.

While they were encamped on the Oxhide the warriors scarcely ever left the delightful place except, of course, when summoned by their chief to the hunt. They sat all day in the shadow of their lodges, puffing lazily at their pipes and relating over and over again the stories of their feats in personal encounters with their enemies, the Cheyennes.

The North American Indians are very assiduous in teaching their boys all that becomes a great warrior, — how to ride the wildest horses, and how to hunt and trap every variety of animal used in the domestic economy of their families. The very moment a son is large enough to handle them, bows and arrows are constantly in his hands.

As the Indians had only a few poor rifles,

whenever Joe went out with his dusky young companions on a hunt, he, too, took nothing but his bow and arrows which the Pawnees had given him, for he did not want his boy friends to feel his superiority when armed with the white man's weapons. The number of squirrels, rabbits, and game birds he killed in a single day would have astonished a city-bred boy.

The Pawnee warriors, flattered by Joe's preference for their society to that of his white neighbors, made him the very finest bows and arrows of which their skill was capable. They looked forward to the day when he should develop into a great warrior, and hoped, too, that the time would come when, becoming tired of civilization, he would let them adopt him into the tribe. One morning, to the surprise of Joe, the old chief despatched a runner back to the reservation with orders to his squaws to make a complete suit of buckskin for his young white friend. In about two weeks when the messenger returned to the camp with the savage dress, Joe, of course, was delighted with his quaint and really beautiful costume. It was made out of the finest doeskin, elegantly embroidered with beads; the seams of the coat-sleeves and trousers were fringed in the most approved savage fashion, while the moccasins were exquisitely wrought with the quills of the porcupine, gayly colored. There were also given the boy all the adjuncts of a warrior, — a tomahawk, medicine-bag, tobacco-pouch, powder-horn, bullet-sack, flint and steel, and, last of all, a magnificent calumet manufactured of the red stone from the sacred quarry in far-off Minnesota.

Joe had never mentioned to any of the family, not even to Rob, what was in store for him from the Pawnees. To make the surprise greater to the household, when he was ready to put on the new suit, he got one of the warriors to decorate his face in royal savage style, and thus metamorphosed, he walked into the cabin one noon, just as the family were about to sit down to dinner. None of them recognized him, and when he began to talk in the Pawnee language, not a word of which any of them could understand, his father motioned him to take a seat at the table and eat, as he had often done to the real Pawnees on their many visits to the ranche.

At last Joe could contain himself no longer, and he cried out in his exultation over the farce he had enacted: " Father, mother, Rob, and you girls, don't you know me ? "

"No!" they all answered simultaneously, but immediately recognizing his voice, now that he spoke English, his mother said that she had never suspected for a moment that the horrid-looking, paint-bedaubed creature before her could be her own child.

Then all had a good laugh over the manner in which Joe had deceived them, but his father insisted that he must go and wash the paint from his face before he thought of sitting down to eat with Christian people; he could allow it in the case of a real savage, because they did not know any better.

Joe was very hungry, for he had been out hunting grouse on the hills all the morning, and was tired, too, so he hastily obeyed his father's injunction. He ran to the spring, and by vigorously rubbing at the various colors, he at last succeeded in getting his face clean. In a few moments he returned to the dining-room looking like himself again, but very stately, by reason of his brand-new suit; and the family could not help staring at and admiring him. Then, when he had taken his place at the table, he was obliged to tell how he had happened to acquire such a fantastic dress, and explain the use of each curious article belonging to it.

Gertrude and Kate both hoped that he would not wear the handsome clothes every day, and his mother suggested that he must never go to the village in such a savage dress. His father said nothing, but evidently regarded his boy with pride.

In reply to the various comments, Joe told the family that he intended to wear the Indian costume only on extraordinary occasions. If ever the Cheyennes, Kiowas, Comanches, or Arapahoes broke out, he would certainly wear it, for when those savages saw him, they would think he was a great warrior, and be careful how they bothered him. The family little thought, as he uttered his playful remarks, how soon that uniform would be worn on a mission fraught with danger to themselves and the whole settlement.

CHAPTER VI

THE family had lived on their comfortable
ranche on the Oxhide for nearly three years.
During the whole of this period the valley had
been most happily exempt from any raid by
the hostile Indians farther west, who for all
that time had made incursions into the sparse
settlements not a hundred miles away, devasta-
ting the country from Nebraska on the north
to the border of Texas on the south.

General Sheridan had been ordered by the
Government to the command of the Military
Department of the Missouri, with headquarters
at Fort Leavenworth. The already famous
General Custer with his celebrated regiment,
the Seventh United States Cavalry, was sta-

tioned at Fort Harker, recently established on
the Smoky Hill, about four miles from Errolstrath ranche, so the settlers on the Oxhide, and
through the valley, felt comparatively safe from
any possible raid by the savages into that region.

One beautiful Sunday afternoon in the middle of the May following the autumn in which
Joe had received his present of a full Indian
dress from the friendly Pawnees, the family
were sitting on the veranda of the cabin.
Dinner was long since over, and Mr. Thompson was reading aloud from their weekly relig-
ious journal, when a horseman suddenly appeared, coming toward the ranche on the trail
which led from the mouth of the Oxhide where
it empties into the Smoky Hill. He was hat-
less and coatless, his long hair was streaming
in the wind, and his heels were rapping his
horse's flanks vigorously, and its breast and
shoulders were covered with foam from the
desperate gait at which it was urged.

The reading was instantly suspended, and
every eye strained toward the unusual object
coming toward the house at such a breakneck
speed.

"I wonder who that is, and why he rides so fast," inquired Mr. Thompson, addressing himself to no one in the group in particular.

"Something unusual must have occurred," suggested Mrs. Thompson; "some one of the neighbors taken ill suddenly, maybe."

"It's no one we know," spoke up Joe. "I never saw that man before," the individual under discussion having come near enough now for his features to be distinguished, "nor the horse he's on, and I know every man and horse in the whole settlement. There's some trouble not far away, I think, or he would not run his animal that way."

In less than three minutes more, the stranger horseman rode up to the front of the house and jumped off his horse. Hurriedly tying him to the hitching-post, he ran up the steps of the veranda, and in the most excited manner, his eyes wearing a wild look and his breath coming with great difficulty, told Mr. Thompson, who had walked forward to meet him, that the Indians had completely destroyed the little settlement of Spillman Creek that morning about daylight. He alone, as far as he knew, had escaped the massacre. He said that luckily he happened to be down in the timber, getting some wood for his morning fire, and the savages did not see him. He had his pony with him, and when he saw the Indians all dressed in their war-bonnets and hideously painted, he rode to the river and across country as fast as his animal could carry him.

"How many families are there in the settlement?" inquired Mr. Thompson.

"About ten," answered the stranger; "forty individuals, perhaps, and all of them, I feel satisfied, have been murdered and their cabins burnt, because I saw the smoke and flames from the trail on the south side of the Saline as I rode hurriedly on."

"Had you no family?" asked Mrs. Thompson, excitedly, in her sympathy for the unfortunate people who had been so cruelly massacred.

"No, ma'am," answered the stranger. "I was living all alone on my claim, which I had taken up only a week ago, on the edge of the timber. My family are still back in Illinois, thank God! or they, too, with myself, would have been butchered with the rest, for I would never have left them."

"Do you think the savages will continue on their raid, and come further down the Saline valley?" inquired Mr. Thompson, who now for the first time since he had been on his ranche, felt a little alarmed for his family.

"I don't know," was the reply, "but I'm afraid they will. The Elkhorn is fairly settled, but the cabins are widely scattered; the Indians know that, and before the neighbors could rally for mutual defence, the savages might be able to murder them in detail. I have come down here to warn the settlers on this creek, and if I can, to get a party to go to the rescue of those on the Elkhorn. I stopped at Fort Harker on my way and reported to the commanding officer the state of affairs, but he said that he had only part of a company of infantry at the post, all the cavalry being out under General Custer, looking after the Indians 'way up the Smoky Hill. He suggested that I should come here to inform you people of the danger, and that, if I could muster up a crowd of men, he would furnish all the arms and ammunition necessary for them. He also said that General Sheridan was coming to Fort Harker in a few days to establish his headquarters there, and that a general Indian war was imminent."

"Have you any idea how many of the savages there were in the band that raided Spillman Creek settlement?" inquired Mr. Thompson.

"I think there must have been about fifty. I counted their pony tracks in the soft mud at the ford of the Saline where they crossed it; they were very plain, and I was enabled to come close to their probable number. If you could muster twenty or thirty men, well armed, who are brave, and good shots with the rifle, I believe that if they start for the Elkhorn to-day, they could circumvent the savages before they reach the creek, or at least drive them out of the neighborhood. I am ready to go back with them and act as guide, for I know every foot of the country, having spent a whole year out there before I settled upon a location. Who are the best men in this settlement, and where shall I go to warn them?"

"Well," replied Mr. Thompson, "I am willing to go for one. I guess there will be no difficulty in gathering as large a force as is necessary — good shots, too; for no one will hesi-

tate a moment when it comes to defending his
family from an Indian raid. It will take a
couple of hours to ride around the neighborhood to the several ranches to notify the men.
My boys, here, can go to the nearest, while you
and I ride to the most remote and get as large
a crowd as possible. Boys," continued he, turning to his sons, who stood with eyes wide open
and mouth agape as they listened with astonishment to the terrible story of the stranger,
"get your ponies at once; saddle them as
quickly as ever you did in your lives, and ride
to the nearest ranches on the creek; up one
side and down the other. Tell all the folks
the dreadful news, and tell them to have the
men meet here at Errolstrath as quickly as they
can, and to bring their rifles with them. All are
well armed," said he, turning to the stranger,
"and they will respond in a hurry."

"Now," said Mr. Thompson, as the boys
jumped off of the veranda to carry out their
father's order, "I will go with you to old Tucker's
ranche. He is a man of most excellent judgment, and a trapper; has fought Indians all his
eventful life on the plains and in the mountains,

so we can safely rely on his advice in regard to what is best to be done." Looking at his wife, he said, "Won't you get this man a bite to eat while I'm catching another animal for him? Yours is tired out," continued he, addressing the stranger again; "you must have a fresh horse. I've got lots of them."

While Mr. Thompson went to the stable, and the stranger to the spring to wash the dust off himself, Mrs. Thompson, assisted by Gertrude and Kate, made ready a cold lunch for the half-famished man, who told them, when he returned to the dining-room, that he had not eaten a morsel since the evening before.

By the time he had finished his meal, Mr. Thompson returned to the front of the house with two animals, and taking the stranger's horse to the stable, after the saddle had been put on the fresh one, he returned to the house. He gave his wife some advice about the boys and their mission, then he and the stranger mounted their animals and loped off at a good gait for the ranche of old Mr. Tucker, three miles away.

The boys had started some while before their father, as it only required a few minutes to catch and saddle their ponies that were pickcted in front of the house, on a patch of buffalo grass not twenty yards away. In less than half an hour they were at the nearest ranche, and had delivered their message. They then rode on and made the rounds of the circuit assigned them, relating the bad news as they travelled from cabin to cabin as quickly as their hardy little Indian ponies could carry them.

While on their mission the boys talked over the story of the massacre, Joe explaining many things in connection with the savage method of making a raid on a white settlement. Those were things which Rob did not fully understand, but with which Joe was familiar, having been told all about them by the friendly Pawnees. He told Rob that he was crazy to go on the little expedition, but did not dare ask permission.

"Father might be willing, maybe," suggested Rob, "though I'm sure that mother and the girls would object."

"I'll bet that I can find the trail of the Cheyennes, for I know better than any one who is going along, that they were Cheyennes who made

the attack," said Joe. "That man who came
down with the news don't know much about
Indians; I could tell that by the way he talked;
he's a 'tender-foot.' He admitted to papa he'd
only been in the country a very short time."

"By jolly! I'll bet he was scared when he saw
those Indians," said Rob; "he wasn't used to
such sights!"

"How he must have ridden his horse," said
Joe. "I never saw an animal so frothy in my
life before; did you, Rob? You could have
scraped a wash-tub of lather off him!"

"If the Cheyennes have left any kind of a trail
after them, I can tell just how many there were
of them," continued Joe, "but they are ahead of
all other Indians in covering up their tracks;
old Yellow Calf has told me so a dozen times. I
expect that it was Charley Bent's band of Dog
soldiers that made the raid."

"What are Dog soldiers?" inquired Rob.

"Why, the young bucks of a tribe who will
not obey the orders of their chief; renegades who
will not be controlled by any custom. Those
Indians who have not done anything yet to make
them warriors, and who go off on their own hook

to murder and steal, and to fire the cabins of the poor settlers, thinking that if they can get a few scalps of women and children they will be recognized by the rest of the tribe as braves. Sometimes there are 'Squaw-men' among them, that is, white men who have married Indian women; generally bad men who have committed some crime where they used to live and dare not go back to where they came from."

"Who is Charley Bent?" asked Rob. "That is not an Indian name, surely!"

"I know it isn't," answered Joe. "He's a half breed; half white and half Cheyenne. His mother was a Cheyenne squaw, and his father was Colonel Bent, one of the most celebrated frontiersmen of his time. Charley was well educated in St. Louis, but when he returned to his father's home, at Bent's Fort, way up the Arkansas River, in what is now Colorado, he threw off the white man's dress and manner of living, joined the Indians, and became, in his devilishness, the worst savage to be found in the whole Indian country. The United States Government has offered a thousand dollars for him, dead or alive. Somebody will catch him yet;

G

the army scouts are after him red hot, so the Pawnees told me."

"I wish the Pawnees, lots of 'em, were back on the creek, Joe," said Rob, continuing the lively conversation they had been keeping up ever since they started from the ranche; "wouldn't they like such a chance to go after their old enemies?"

"I expect they will be here sooner than usual, this coming autumn; one of the boys told me so when the band left; but it will be four months yet before we may look for them."

"Are you going to ask to go with the party to the Elkhorn, Joe?" asked Rob of his brother.

"No, I think not. I intend to be still unless some of the crowd drop a hint they'd like to have me along; then I'll speak out."

By four o'clock the boys returned to the ranche, having warned twelve families of the impending danger. All the men expressed their readiness to go with Mr. Thompson and the others to circumvent the savages on their raid. When Joe and Rob had turned their ponies out to graze and went back to the house again, they found a dozen men there already, waiting for the return of their father and the stranger. The anxious group sat on the veranda, discussing the state of affairs, suggesting to each other what course should be pursued concerning those settlers who would have to remain in the valley with their wives and children. Uncle Dick Smith, as he was familiarly called, an old man with white hair and long white beard, who had had some experience with the savages in his earlier days in Wisconsin, suggested that while the scouting party were absent, Job Wilkersin's stone corral would be the best place for the settlers to rendezvous in case the Indians came down into the valley of the Oxhide. After some discussion, however, it was agreed to let the question remain open until Mr. Thompson and the other men should arrive.

A short time before sundown a group of horsemen could be seen coming down the trail from the north. They were those for whom the crowd at Errolstrath were anxiously looking. When they rode up to the house, headed by Mr. Thompson, they dismounted, fastened their horses to trees, and after a hurried meal which the girls had been getting ready during their father's absence, they all adjourned to the lawn outside

of the veranda, and the subject was renewed
as to what those should do who were compelled
to remain behind on the Oxhide. Mr. Wilkersin
was among them, and as he stated his house was
the largest in the neighborhood, and his big
stone corral a grand place for defence in case the
savages continued on their raid, it was agreed
to rendezvous there. Twenty determined men
in the corral could keep off a hundred Indians,
and besides there was food enough at his house
for every one who should go there. He further
said that he would be glad to assist his friends
thus much in trying times like these.

Rob, who was familiar with the location of
every cabin in the settlement, was immediately
despatched on a fresh horse to call on the people
and communicate the result of the conference.
He was to tell them where to go in the event of
the Indians coming into Oxhide valley after the
scouting party had left for the Elkhorn.

There were about thirty men who were obliged
to remain at home; too old to undertake the
fatigue of the long night's ride contemplated.
They were all excellent shots, many of them having been pioneers in the settlement of the states

east of the Mississippi when they constituted the far West.

When all the men who could be mustered for the expedition had arrived at Errolstrath, there were about fifty. Old man Tucker was unanimously chosen for their leader, with the title, by courtesy, of captain. He was a man nearly sixty-five years old, but had been early recognized by the settlers of the valley as one to whom they could look whenever the affairs of the neighborhood demanded the exercise of good judgment or sound advice. He was well educated, having graduated at Yale, but after graduation a quarrel with his father resulted in his drifting out on the frontier, where his life had been that of a trapper and hunter. He was as active as any of the young men, so his age in this case did not militate against him. He was the best rifle-shot in the valley, and if, like Davy Crockett, he failed to hit a squirrel in the eye, "it didn't count!"

The stranger from Spillman Creek was named Alderdyce, as he had informed Mr. Thompson while on the trip with him, and, as many of those who now met him for the first time desired to hear his story, he related the details of the horrid

massacre again. At its sickening recital a majority became impatient of delay, and wanted to
start on the trail of the savages at once, although
the whole valley was flooded with the golden
glow of sunset.

Joe stood modestly in the crowd, eagerly drinking in the awful story told by Mr. Alderdyce, and
he noticed how anxious the scouting party was
to get away. He knew that this would be the
height of absurdity until night had closed in, and
in all probability would defeat the very object of
the expedition, so he ventured to suggest that it
would be better to wait until after dark.

Old Mr. Tucker knew as well as the boy's
father that Joe's judgment in matters relating to
savage methods when on the war-path was far in
advance of his sixteen years. His ideas and
opinions commanded a consideration his age did
not otherwise warrant, so the keen observation
he had developed since his intimacy with the
Pawnees, and the astuteness he had imbibed from
them, caused Mr. Tucker to ask the boy's rea-
sons for his suggestion.

Joe replied hesitatingly: " I believe it's better
to wait until dark. The runners, as their spies

are called, of the hostile band, are, I honestly
think, at this moment stationed on some of the
highest points of the valley. They are watching
to learn if there will be any demonstration made
against the raiding band from this settlement.
If this is true, and I believe it is, they should
not be permitted to see our party start out. If
they do discover that a number of mounted men
are riding on the prairie, they will hang on their
trail, keep the main band warned of every movement, and you could not effect anything. In
that case you might as well stay at home."

Upon these hints so forcibly thrown out by
Joe, nearly every one at once coincided with his
opinion, and the captain decided to act upon the
boy's judgment.

Joe, who was always an attentive listener,
rarely obtruded his ideas into the conversation
of his elders; in reality he was of rather a reti-
cent disposition, a trait generally indicative of
bravery, but he was ever ready to venture an
opinion when asked for it, fearlessly and in great
earnestness. So during the discussion of the
supposed details of the morning's massacre, Captain Tucker asked him what he thought of the

probability of the savages coming down to the
Elkhorn from the scene of their raid on the
Spillman.

"Well, Mr. Tucker," replied Joe, "distance is
never considered by an Indian. If a band start
on a raid and are successful at the beginning,
they will keep on a dozen miles or five hundred;
it makes no difference to them; they'll wear out
any animal but a wolf. If the massacre was complete, as Mr. Alderdyce thinks, they will probably
keep right on murdering, scalping, and firing the
cabins, until they get a setback. My own opinion is that they will go down to the Elkhorn
or some other place where there is a settlement,
and if successful again, will continue on and
come to the Oxhide, perhaps, now they have
tasted blood. But if they have met with a
repulse anywhere, or learn that the United States
troops are after them, they may abandon their
raid and be now a hundred miles on the trail
to their village."

Joe was evidently fidgety; he wanted to go
along, and as the captain and his father had
questioned him so earnestly on such important
matters, he thought he had a right to be one of

the party; still, he said nothing until Captain Tucker, noticing the boy's anxious countenance, asked him if he would like to go with them.

Joe answered very quickly in the affirmative, but it was with much hesitancy that his parents gave their consent. The neighbors gathered at the ranche, however, importuned very earnestly in his favor, declaring that the success of the expedition might depend materially upon their decision whether the boy should go or not. Of course, to resist such an appeal was out of the question, coming as it did almost unanimously from their friends, so Joe was permitted to accompany the party.

Hurriedly did the delighted boy go out to the corral and saddle his favorite pony, a coal-black little animal, very swift, full of endurance, sure-footed as a mule, and as obedient to the touch of its young master's hand and legs as a well-trained circus horse. Soon returning, he tied him with the other animals to a tree and then went into the house to prepare himself for the venturesome trip.

Coming back on the veranda in a few moments dressed in the buckskin suit given him by the old chief Yellow Calf, he looked the very im-

personation of a veteran frontiersman, and but
for his childish face might have passed for a
veritable army scout. He slung his rifle across
the horn of his saddle; its complement of bullets
in his pouch he fastened to the cantle, while the
powder-flask was suspended by a cord thrown
over his shoulder. He also carried his flint and
steel, thinking he might have occasion to use it,
and with a small lantern was ready for whatever
he might be called upon to do.

As the welcome darkness would not come for
an hour yet, the party kept their animals concealed in the thick timber near the cabin. They
sat quietly in the shadow of the veranda, so that
if there were any of the hostile spies in the vicinity, as Joe had suggested there might be; they
would not be able to observe any unusual demonstration on the place, as the house was completely masked by the giant trees surrounding it.

By eight o'clock it was dark enough to venture
out, and the party quietly mounted their horses,
and strung out in single file down the narrow
trail leading from the ranche to the ford of the
Smoky Hill. Tucker, Joe, and Alderdyce were
at the head of the line. Every one was familiar

with the trail as far as the river, for it was the main travelled track to the village of Ellsworth. It was six miles from Errolstrath, and contained a general store, a blacksmith shop, and the post office for all the surrounding country.

The ford crossed the Smoky Hill about two miles east of the little hamlet, but the party did not follow the trail up the river. They took a shorter cut over the hills bordering the stream where there was a series of buffalo paths running northward in the direction they wanted to go. They thus saved a détour of three or four miles, an important consideration where time was of the greatest consequence. The buffalo paths all came out on the other side of the high divide separating the Saline from the Smoky Hill. A short distance beyond the summit of the ridge, and down a gradual slope, was one of the valleys of the several tributaries which gave the many-branched stream called the Elkhorn, its suggestive name.

After the party had forded the Smoky Hill, the country was unknown to all excepting Alderdyce and Joe. The latter had often accompanied the Pawnees on their hunts as far as the Saline and Paradise creeks, twenty-five miles from the Oxhide.

All had been travelling up to that point in groups of twos and threes on the flat river bottom, but now again they strung out in Indian file, following Joe and Alderdyce slowly up the divide and down on the other side. They then all moved out more rapidly into a short, quick lope as the ground was more level for several miles. At the end of the level stretch they halted, as they were approaching the beginning of the limestone region.

Following Joe's advice they dismounted and muffled the hoofs of their horses with gunny sacks which they had brought for that purpose, in order to prevent the sound of the animals' feet from being heard by any of the savage runners.

This wise precaution was frequently employed by the scouts of the army with General Sheridan during his celebrated winter campaign against the allied tribes of the plains, when the troops were obliged to travel at night through the enemy's country.

It was soon after they had passed the limestone region that a heavy rolling prairie, over which the trail ran up one slope and down another of the rocky divides, separated the narrow intervales between. Most of the time it was a hard, killing pace for the poor horses, as they had travelled for hours continuously without a halt, excepting to muffle their feet. The settlement must be reached before daylight, or perhaps it would be too late to thwart the murderous schemes of the Indians, who always chose the early hours of the dawn in which to commit their atrocities. At that time when sleep oppresses most heavily, life and death were the issue, and the tired animals could not be mercifully spared. Would they be able to hold out with ten miles of the same cruel lope ahead of them, before the breaks of the main Elkhorn would be reached?

There was an hour more of severe riding, during which the heels of the riders and the sharp sting of the quirt were often called into requisition to urge the jaded animals on to their hard duty. They were flecked with foam, their nostrils distended, and they were almost worn out when the terribly earnest men rode down the last divide into the grassy bottom of the first branch of the main Elkhorn.

The faintest streaks of the coming dawn were beginning to show themselves; the summits of the Twin Mounds, capped with white limestone, already reflected the rosy tinge of the rising sun, which was still far below the horizon of the valley. The beautiful intervales, through which the party urged their horses, were covered with buffalo grass, and at the farther end, not quite half a mile distant, the fringe of timber bordering the creek could be distinguished as its dark contour cast a still blacker shadow over the sombre valley.

There the party halted for a few moments to reconnoitre. Captain Tucker again had occasion to interrogate Joe. He inquired of the young trailer what would be the first acts of the savages when they arrived in the valley of the Elkhorn, if indeed they came at all.

" Well, Mr. Tucker," replied the boy, " the first thing the Indians would do — they'd hide themselves in the timber; lie down in the grass, probably, and then send out one or more of their runners, the very best they had with them, to sneak around and watch for a chance to make a break together on the cabins. Then, if the outlook was favorable, and none of the settlers were stirring, they'd go from cabin to cabin, murdering, scalping, and firing the buildings as fast as they could."

"Well, then," said the captain, as he took both of the boy's hands in his own, and gazed into his bright face, "you know that all the settlers on the Oxhide, and your own folks, too, say that you are as much of an Indian as if you had been born in a tepee, so far as savage education is concerned. Now, I've been talking to your father, and he agrees with me; I want you to do some dangerous work, or at least it is somewhat risky. You are the only one among us all who can do it as it should be done. It is this. While we remain here in the shadow of the timber to blow our animals and graze them a little, I want you to cross the creek on foot, and go up to Spillman Ford with Alderdyce, who will show you where it intersects this branch of the Elkhorn, and try to discover, if you can, by the dim light, any signs of Indians. I'm inclined to think they have not come down into this valley at all. But I want you to find out where they are, if possible. If you do not find any track of them, after we have rested our horses and warned the settlers of the danger, we will all go on to the scene of the massacre, and there you will be sure to learn where they have gone."

Joe and Alderdyce turned over their horses to one of the men who were on guard watching the animals while they fed on the rich buffalo grass, and then started on foot for the ford of the Elkhorn leading to Spillman Creek. It was about a mile, and during the walk, Joe and Alderdyce talked over the affair of the morning. Joe asked his companion to tell him exactly what the commanding officer had said to him when he reported the massacre to him at Fort Harker.

"Well, Joe, I will tell you just what he told me. He said that General Sheridan had ordered a company of Custer's regiment of mounted troopers to be sent to the Elkhorn valley and to remain there until the settlers were advised to come in, or the proposed Indian war was ended."

"Now I have an idea," said Joe to him. "We shall not find any Indians on this trip; the cavalry have already started for the valley, and the savages have got wind of it and have gone back to their village, probably, a hundred miles south of the Arkansas. But, anyhow, we'll go on up to the ford and learn what we can."

When they reached the crossing, not a sign of a pony's hoof could be discovered, and both gave a sigh of relief as they now knew that none of the savages had come down towards the Elkhorn. They hurried back to their party, and Joe reported that he had not seen a sign.

"Good enough," said Captain Tucker, as he listened to the good news. "Now, men," continued he, turning and addressing himself to the party who had gathered near him to learn what report Joe and Alderdyce might bring, "we will remain here for another hour, and after warning some of the prominent settlers in the valley, we will go up to the head of Spillman Creek and see what is to be discovered there. Who knows but some one may be found hidden in the brush, not daring to come out. We may be able to save a life or two yet."

H

CHAPTER VII

JUST as the sun appeared above the top of
the Twin Mounds, Joe, who could not keep
quiet when among the timber or on the prairie,
was scouting around on his own hook, while the
remainder of the party was lying on the grass
eating the cold breakfast they had brought from
Errolstrath. Suddenly he rushed down to them,
and yelled at the top of his voice : —

"The cavalry are coming! I saw the gleam
of their carbines on the ridge about a mile
away toward the trail to Fort Harker."

Every man was on his feet in an instant;
and sure enough, in a few minutes they heard
the clanging of sabres and the sound of the
hoofs of approaching horses. Presently a fine-

looking set of men wearing the fatigue uniform of the United States Cavalry, splendidly
mounted on sleek bay animals, swung around
the point of timber where Captain Tucker and
his scouts from the Oxhide valley were standing. The trumpeter sounded the "Halt," and
in another moment the horses, in obedience to
the signal, stood still as if petrified, while the
commander of the troop, Colonel Keogh, of
Custer's famous regiment, rode forward and
talked with Captain Tucker, whom he had at
once recognized as the leader of the scouts.

They conversed for some moments, each giving the other what information he had of the
movements of the Indians. Then the Colonel
told Captain Tucker that his orders were to
camp on the Elkhorn with his company, and
scout through the valley, protecting the settlers.
He said that a detachment of infantry was also
ordered to the creek, and was to remain there,
while he with his mounted men would move
from point to point, and thus prevent the savages from making another raid in that part of
the country. He thanked Captain Tucker for
the promptness with which he and his neighbors

had responded to the appeal of Alderdyce. He
said that now the cavalry were there the men
might go home feeling assured that no more
attacks were to be feared from the Indians, and
that General Sheridan would soon have enough
soldiers under his command to whip thoroughly
the allied tribes, and force them to a peace
which they would be glad to keep.

Captain Tucker told the Colonel how bright
Joe was in relation to Indian affairs, and what
a great hunter he had already become. After
Colonel Keogh had himself conversed with Joe,
he took a great fancy to him. He told him
that he was going on a deer hunt just as soon
as he was settled in camp, and the infantry had
arrived, and he invited Joe to be one of the
party.

Joe thanked the Colonel, and spoke modestly
of the compliments which had been paid him by
Captain Tucker. He promised that he would
certainly go on the hunt with him, and be delighted to do so.

He spoke up boldly: "When do you expect
to go, Colonel? I know there are lots of red
deer and elk, too, on the Elkhorn, and this is

a good time to find them; I've been here with the Pawnees often."

The Colonel said: " The infantry, in all probability, will reach the creek some time this evening, as they were getting ready for the march when I left Fort Harker with my troop. Suppose, Joe, we say the day after to-morrow? You can remain here with me; I have buffalo robes, and you shall have a bed in my tent. So go and ask your father at once and come back to me as quick as you can and report his answer. You'll find me somewhere about the camp. My tent is not yet put up, but you will know it when it is, by its similarity to an Indian tepee. It is called a 'Sibley,' and was patterned after the Sioux lodge by its inventor, an officer of the army of that name."

Joe, wild with delight, ran off to find his father, to whom he told of the invitation, and finding that no objections were made, thanked him for his permission to remain.

Captain Tucker had informed the Colonel that as his men and animals were sufficiently rested, and the horses filled with the rich grass, he intended to go to the scene of the massacre with Alderdyce, to find whether any of the settlers were hiding and not daring to show themselves, or if any of the wounded were still living. Should he find any of the latter, he would return by way of Fort Harker and notify the commanding officer, so that he might send an ambulance for them and medical assistance.

Telling his men of his intentions, they immediately brought in their horses and saddled them. They then mounted, and rode slowly west toward Spillman Creek, which was about seven or eight miles from the Elkhorn. Joe, of course, went with them, as they wanted him to find out which way the Indians had gone after committing their devilish deeds. He intended to leave the party at the ford of the Elkhorn on its return, and to join Colonel Keogh.

In about two hours the party arrived at the mouth of Spillman Creek, and the first evidence of the acts of the savages confronted the men. Riding up to a small cabin which the Indians had not consigned to the torch, no doubt having missed it on their fiendish rounds, they discovered two little girls crouched in one of its dark corners. One of them was only six years old, and

her sister but eight. They were very bright for
their age, and told a wonderfully sad story of
their escape from the Indians. They said that a
big band of savages rode up to their home very
early in the morning; that their father and
mother were not yet out of bed. The Indians
killed both of them, and after setting the house
on fire, threw the children on their ponies and
rode off. Coming to the top of a high hill, they
saw a company of soldiers in the distance, and
they then dropped them on the prairie and hurried away as fast as their ponies could run. The
girls were not hurt at all. They wandered on,
frightened nearly to death, and seeing the cabin
down in the valley, they went to it and slept there
all night. They had waked very early in the
morning, and on going out of doors, saw the wild
grapes growing on the vines at the creek; they
ate some for their breakfast, but soon hearing the
sound of horses' hoofs, and thinking the Indians
were coming to look for them, they crawled back
into the corner where the scouts had found them.

Captain Tucker and the rest of the scouts were
in a dilemma at first when they found themselves
with the two little orphaned children on their

hands; and they did not know exactly what to do. But soon Joe's excellent judgment manifested itself. He proposed that one of the men should be sent back to Colonel Keogh's camp to tell him of their discovery, and ask him to send his ambulance out to take the children to Fort Harker, where they would be cared for by the kind ladies of the post.

The suggestion was acted upon at once. Every man volunteered to go, so it was left to the Captain to select one. This he did, started him off, and left Mr. Thompson to stay with the little girls until the arrival of the ambulance. He and the others of the party then rode up on the valley of Spillman Creek, as the savages appeared to have confined their atrocities to that narrow region.

As they were riding close to the bank of the stream, about three miles from where they had found the two girls, they saw a wagon with the horses still attached. As they came up to it for a closer examination, two men, both of whom were known to Alderdyce, came out of the underbrush.

They had a story to tell, too. Early in the

morning they were on their way to examine a
claim on the Spillman, when they perceived at
only a short distance from them, what appeared
to be a body of soldiers. They were all dressed
in blue blouses, and were marching four abreast
just as the cavalry do. The men stopped for a
moment to get a closer view as they rode up the
divide, when to their horror they discovered the
supposed soldiers to be a band of Indians. They
turned their team about, and made for the nearest
timber on the creek and hid themselves. Next
morning they still decided to remain in ambush
until they saw some white people. They had
plenty of food with them, so they had remained
until they were discovered by Captain Tucker's
scouts. Learning that all was safe, they climbed
into their wagon, whipped up the team, and drove
away. Presently the scouts came to the remains
of a cabin, partly destroyed by fire, where they
discovered the dead bodies of a man and woman,
probably husband and wife. These they decently
buried and rode on.

They next found the body of a young man,
dead in his field, where he had evidently been at
work when the savages surprised him. He was

murdered with his own hatchet, which was found
by his side, his face having been chopped until
it was not recognizable.   His body was interred
too.

It is useless to relate all that the scouts saw
on their mission of discovery up the Spillman.
In all, thirty bodies were found, and some dozen
or more persons who had been wounded and had
managed to hide after the savages had supposed
them to be dead.   During the next twenty-four
hours these were gathered and taken to the
hospital at the fort.   Some recovered, but the
majority died.

The party returned to Colonel Keogh's camp,
because they had discovered so much that it was
thought best he should know.   When they arrived there they learned that the little girls had
been sent to the fort under an escort of a squad
of the troopers, and they also found Mr. Thompson in the camp waiting for them.

After winding their horses for about half an
hour, all returned to Errolstrath, with the exception of Joe, who remained to go on the proposed
hunt when the infantry arrived.

Colonel Keogh's tent was already pitched,

and Joe sat in there with him discussing the atrocities on Spillman Creek and the deer hunt.

"Colonel," said Joe, "you know that deer have no gall-bladder and the antelope no dew-claws. Did you ever hear the Indian legend about the reason?"

"I know the deer have no gall-bladder and the antelope no dew-claws, but I don't think I have ever heard the reason. What do the Indians say about it, Joe?"

"Well, old Yellow Calf, the chief of the band of Pawnees which has camped on our creek ever since we have lived there, told me that a long time ago a deer and an antelope met on the prairie near the Great Bend of the Arkansas. At that time both animals had a gall and dew-claws. They fell to talking together and bragging how fast each could run. The deer claimed that he could outstrip the antelope, and the antelope that he could beat the deer. They got awfully mad at each other, and finally determined they would try their speed. The stakes were their galls, and the trial was made on the open prairie. The antelope beat the deer and took the deer's gall. The deer felt very unhappy at his defeat, and he became so miserable over it, that the antelope felt sorry for him, and to cheer him up took off both his dew-claws and gave them to the deer. Ever since then the deer has had no gall-bladder, and the antelope no dew-claws.

"I met some Kaws once, and I told them what the Pawnees had told me about it, and the chief of that band said the story the Pawnees had told was only partly correct. The Kaw chief's version was that after the antelope had won the race, the deer said to him, 'You have won, but that race was not fair, for it was over the prairie. We ought to try again in the woods to decide which of us is really the faster.' So the antelope agreed to run the second race, and on it they bet their dew-claws. The deer beat the antelope that time, because he could run faster than the antelope through the timber, over the fallen trunks of trees, and in the thick underbrush, and he took the antelope's dew-claws."

"Well, Joe, that is a very funny story; I never heard it before." Then, looking out of the front of his tent, the Colonel turned to Joe, and said,

"There comes the company of infantry, so we may go on our hunt to-morrow."

Joe ran out and watched the infantry as they filed into the timber. It was after sundown, but far from dark. The men were soon settled in their tents, their camp-kettles bubbling over the fires, and preparations in full swing for their evening meal.

Joe wandered among the troops and soon picked up an acquaintance with them. They admired his Indian suit, and earnestly listened to the tale of his adventures with the Pawnees. Presently he was called by the Colonel's orderly to come to supper. He went back to the Sibley tent, where he sat down at the table with Colonel Keogh and his two lieutenants.

Their simple table was improvised out of the end gates of two of the wagons, and the cook, a colored soldier, had managed to provide an excellent meal, and as Joe was very hungry, he did ample justice to it.

When the trumpets and the bugles sounded the retreat, Joe went out with the Colonel, who inspected the men to see that everything was in good order for the night. They then returned

to their canvas quarters, where the Colonel
smoked his pipe, and again discussed to-morrow's
hunt with the boy.

They were to make a very early start in the
morning, so, as soon as "taps" had sounded,
which meant that all lights must be put out and
the soldiers retire to their tents, the Colonel
suggested to Joe that he had better go to bed,
while he would sit up a while and write out his
report to the commander at Fort Harker. Call-
ing in the orderly, the Colonel told him to fix up
a sleeping-place for the boy. The man spread
four heavy buffalo robes on the floor of the tent,
and putting two blankets on top, the bed was
ready for Joe, who tumbled into it and was soon
fast asleep.

When the trumpeter sounded the reveille, at
the first streak of dawn the next morning, the
Colonel, who had already risen, called Joe, who
bounded out of his soft bed like a cat. Breakfast
was ready in a few moments, and after he and the
Colonel had eaten, and the latter had given his
orders to the officer who was to command the
camp during his absence, Joe and he started out
on foot for the hunt.

The night had been cold, and although it was the middle of May, the white rime of the late frost covered the earth.   It was a good omen, as the sharp footprints of the animals could be more easily distinguished.

Carefully examining their rifles and cartridges as they walked briskly on, they soon struck the main branch of the Elkhorn, and continued along its margin in a southerly direction for a mile or more, when they came to a little opening.

There Joe suddenly stopped, and turning to Colonel Keogh, who had on the instant also halted, said, " Doesn't that look a little deerish, Colonel ? "

The Colonel, though a good shot and hunter, could distinguish nothing out of the ordinary after scrutinizing the ground to which the boy had pointed.   The earth looked the same everywhere in the Colonel's eyes.

" Here ! " said Joe, as, noticing the bewildered appearance of his new friend, he turned over a fallen cottonwood leaf with his foot.   There the Colonel saw, after carefully stooping down, the very faint impress of a hoof.

"Is that a fresh track, Joe ? " he asked.

"You may be sure it is," replied Joe, "and only about an hour old!"

"Well, I want *that* deer," said Colonel Keogh, enthusiastically.   He rose from a stump on which he had been sitting for a few moments, with his rifle across his knees, and started quickly for a little patch of box-elder not a hundred yards distant.

"Hold on, Colonel!" said Joe, cautiously; "the deer isn't there now. Don't you see his hoof-marks point the other way? Look, here's where he's nibbled the grass," pointing with his rifle to a strip of bunch-grass in the opposite direction from the box-elders. "Let's go on, Colonel; deer don't stay long in one spot so early in the day, and if we don't get a move on us, it may be hours before we can get a shot at 'em."

They trudged on for about a mile and a half, walking side by side, the Colonel telling the boy some of his experiences in the war of the Rebellion. Suddenly Joe, touching the Colonel's shoulder, said, "Hark!" in a hoarse whisper, at the same instant elevating his head like a stag-hound that has just winded game.   In

another minute they heard a rustling as though
something were stepping on dead leaves.

"There's a buck deer in there, and a big one,
too," said Joe, in a whisper, as he pointed to a
bunch of upland willows whose slender tops were
oscillating slowly as if disturbed by a gentle
breeze, though there was not a breath of wind
blowing. "He's probably got a half dozen or
more does around him, and if we are mighty
careful, we may both get a shot."

The willow copse was on the top of a little
knoll, and the ground was smooth on the side
of it where the Colonel and Joe stood. Here
and there at intervals were great trees, but without any underbrush to snap under their feet as
they quietly trod over the soft, black soil.

At Joe's suggestion, he and the Colonel separated, widening the distance between them to
about twenty paces, Colonel Keogh on the right
of Joe. They crept on as silently as savages on
the trail of an enemy, and soon arrived at the
base of the elevation, which was only some fifty
yards to its crest. There they noticed that the
dark earth had been cut up in every direction by
the sharp, delicate foot-marks of the creatures

1

supposed to be in front of them. A significant glance rapidly passed from one to the other as they drew nearer their quarry.

At that juncture, just as they reached the edge of the copse, each masked himself behind a good-sized cottonwood, which seemed to have grown where it did for their especial use. The Colonel in his enthusiasm could not repress the remark in a whisper to Joe : —

" Look there, Joe.   There's a dozen deer ! "

Sure enough, right in front of them were a dozen fat does lying down ruminating their morning meal. The old buck, the guardian of the whole herd, was standing up as if watching over his charge, and stamping the ground with his sharp hoofs to drive off the buffalo gnats that swarmed thickly around him.

In another instant, at a signal previously agreed upon, a low whistle from the Colonel, the rifles of the hunters were discharged simultaneously, and all but two of the terribly frightened animals bounded off through the timber.

Before the echoes of the pieces had died away, Joe was among the struggling deer with his hunting-knife, cutting their throats while they

were yet in their death throes. The stately
buck had been the Colonel's game, and he asked
Joe to take its head to the ranche so that the
Pawnees, when they arrived in the autumn, could
preserve it with its magnificent set of antlers,
which he desired to keep as a trophy of their
hunt.

It was but a little more than two miles to camp,
and they did not have to wait more than an hour
for a wagon to arrive, as the driver had been told
by the Colonel to start the moment the sharp
double report of the rifles reached his ears. The
dead animals were soon loaded into it, and the
proud hunters walked leisurely alongside of it,
back to camp, arriving there before eleven
o'clock.

The deer were skinned by Joe. The meat was
cut up into saddles and haunches, and hung on
the limb of a great tree, to secure it from the
prowling wolves, who already scented blood and
began to make their appearance on the bluffs, so
keen is the nose of that vicious and cowardly
brute. The Colonel had brought with him from
the fort, half a dozen hounds, among them some
of General Custer's celebrated animals, but they

were left tied up in camp that morning, as the Colonel had decided to make a still hunt the first day, and to chase with the dogs the next.

That evening, just as all were about to roll themselves up in their blankets, a scout arrived from Fort Harker with the intelligence that the Cheyennes and the Kiowas, under the leadership of the bloodthirsty Sa-tan-ta, the notorious war-chief, had made a raid upon the settlements near Council Grove, and Custer was leaving at once for the field with his regiment. As Colonel Keogh's company was part of it, he must return to Fort Harker immediately, and another detachment of colored infantry were on their way to take its place on the Elkhorn.

All was bustle in a few moments. Tents were struck, and in less than an hour the cavalry command was on its way, Joe riding at the head of the column with the Colonel.

They arrived at Fort Harker long before daylight, and Joe bade the Colonel good by and rode on to Errolstrath, where he pulled up his pony just as his father and Rob were coming out of the house to go to the spring to wash themselves.

The boy was gladly welcomed back by all the family, and they sat at the table for more than an hour after they finished eating their breakfast, listening to Joe's experiences at the scene of the massacre, and his hunt with Colonel Keogh.

CHAPTER VIII

MR. TUCKER PASSES THE NIGHT AT ERROLSTRATH — HE TELLS SOME
STORIES OF HUNTING BIG GAME IN THE ROCKY MOUNTAINS —
SAGACITY OF THE FEMALE BIGHORN — THE AMERICAN COUGAR
— THE BEAR AND THE PANTHER — THE RABBIT HUNT — HOW
THE BOYS TRAINED THEIR HOUNDS.

THAT evening many of those who had acted
as scouts under Captain Tucker came to Errolstrath, where, on the shady veranda they discussed their trip and the possibilities of a
prolonged Indian war. The Kiowas had inaugu-
rated hostilities by their raid on the settlements
near Council Grove. General Sheridan had
already established his headquarters at Fort
Harker, and every preparation was going on at
that post for a winter campaign against the
allied tribes.

After the group on the porch had talked matters over for about two hours, they all went to
their respective homes excepting old Mr. Tucker,
whom the family had invited to stay all night.

As it was but eight o'clock when the others left, Joe and Mr. Tucker turned to the subject of hunting big game, and the latter told some of his own adventures when he was a trapper in the Rocky Mountains many years ago. As Joe had never seen the bighorn of that region, Mr. Tucker related an adventure he once had when hunting for a pair of young ones. He was up in the Yellowstone Range, not very far from the scene of Custer's unequal battle with Sitting Bull, in which the General's entire command was annihilated by the savages.

" My camp was on the Green River," began the old man, " and one morning while I was out baiting my traps, I noticed a she bighorn that I knew would soon have little ones. I was determined to have a pair of kids, as I had a sort of a small menagerie at my camp, but it contained no bighorn. So I started to follow her trail and stay with her until her kids were born, when I intended to capture them and make pets of them.

" I followed her for about two weeks, and was sometimes compelled to creep cautiously after her in my stockinged feet. My stockings were clumsy

things made of buckskin, not such stockings as
you buy. One evening being so near her, and
obliged to climb a steep mountain, I took out my
knife and cut off all the silver trimmings of my
buckskin suit, so that nothing could jingle and
scare her.

"At last, after tracking her day after day, I
came upon her den, where she had brought forth
two kids. It was the very top of one of the tallest peaks in the Wind River Mountains, in a sort
of cave about five feet deep, worn in the side of
an enormous rock. When I first got a sight of
the kids, they were nearly two weeks old, and
were jumping and playing as all of the goat or
sheep family are wont to do.

" They were alone, but their mother was on
the brink of a precipice, within a hundred yards
of them, carefully looking down into the valley
below to see if she could discover anything hostile. They are great watchers. The old one had
not seen me, and I had made a détour to the very
summit of the mountain, where I could see that
there was a trail which the mother used to travel
in going to and from her young ones. I felt
sure that once at the mouth of the cave or hole

in the big rock, I might easily capture the kids, for which I had footed it so many miles and followed so many days.

"Before I reached the entrance of the den the old one caught a glimpse of me, and in an instant, filled with the courage which the maternal instinct always prompts, she was upon me and trying to get the sharp point of her crooked horns into my legs to toss me over the precipice which formed one of the walls of the mountain. The trail on which I was standing was narrow and slippery. I had left my rifle on the top of the divide, and was in a mighty tight place, for the female bighorn is almost as dangerous as a tiger when enraged and solicitous for the safety of her little ones.

"I fought off the infuriated mother with my hands and feet as well as I could, but the rage of the brute increased terribly every second. Just then she caught sight of her kids, and leaving me, she rushed toward them and ran around them several times, as if telling them she wanted them to do something in her great trouble.

"The distance from the wall of one mountain to the precipice of the other was but eight feet.

Both had originally been but one mountain, but ages ago some great convulsion of nature had split them apart, and had left a huge fissure between them at least two thousand feet deep, with walls as smooth as glass.

"The old one ran back and forth from the precipice to the kids several times, showing them as plainly as if she could talk that they must make the leap to escape from their natural enemy. At last, as if the whole matter was understood, the mother flew back to the edge of the cañon, the little ones hot in her tracks, and then all three made the jump, just clearing the frightful gorge by half the length of the young ones.

"I was dumfounded for an instant, but soon recovered my senses and went for my rifle, but the coveted animals were far out of range on the top of the twin peak. I then returned to my camp on Green River more than a hundred miles away, disgusted and worn out, and never again attempted to capture the kids of the bighorn in the fashion of my first venture."

Joe and the rest of the family, remembering Joe's scrap with the young panther, asked the old man if he had ever had any fight with one of them. He said that he had, and would tell them all about it. Then they would go to bed, as it was very late for the ranche folks to be up.

"I remember the day you had that tussle with a young panther, Joe, and I tell you that you got off mighty luckily; the chances were that the animal would have made mincemeat of you if it hadn't been for that thrust with your knife.

"The California lion, puma, or panther, as the animal is indifferently called according to locality, once had a very extensive range on the North American continent. It could be found from the Adirondacks to Patagonia, but now, like nearly all of our indigenous great mammals, is relatively scarce, and is rapidly following the sad trail of the buffalo.

"Although sometimes called a lion, he in nowise resembles either his African or Asiatic namesake. He is more nearly related to the tiger in his habits, though lion-like in color. He is the puma or American cougar of the naturalists. He is really a long-tailed cat, and the only true representative of the genus felis on the continent.

"He is a splendid fellow, too, with sleepy green eyes, skin as soft as velvet and beautifully mottled, and teeth half an inch long and sharp as razors. His paws measure four inches across, and his limbs are as finely proportioned as a sculptor could desire, while all his muscles are as brawny as a prize-fighter's. His breast is broad, and his body as flexible as a snake's. He is an active climber and generally drops or springs upon his prey from a limb where he has carefully secreted himself. Like the majority of wild beasts, he generally runs from man, excepting when cornered, or in the case of a female with kittens when suddenly met; then her motherly love presents itself as strongly as in any other animal.

"The cougar attains its greatest size in the Rocky Mountains, where its body reaches a length of four feet ten inches, and its tail from two to two and a half feet.

"The American panther has one inveterate foe, the bear. The grizzly and the panther are mortal enemies. The famous trappers I have

known, such men as Kit Carson and Lucien
B. Maxwell, have told me that in these animals' frequent combats, the panther generally
comes out victor, and that in their early trapping days they often came across the carcass
of a bear which had evidently met its death in
a lively encounter with a mountain lion, as
they called it.

"Carson once related a contest of that character which he had accidentally witnessed. A
large deer was running at full speed, closely
followed by a panther. The chase had already
been a long one, for as they came nearer to
where he stood, he could see both of their
parched tongues hanging out of their mouths,
and their bounding, though powerful, was no
longer as elastic as usual. The deer having
discovered in the distance a large black bear
playing with her cub, stopped for a moment to
sniff the air, then coming nearer, he made a
bound with head extended, to ascertain whether
the bear had kept her position. As the panther was closing with him, the deer wheeled
sharply around, and turning almost upon its
own trail, passed within thirty yards of its pur-

suer. The panther, not being able at once to stop his career, gave an angry growl and followed the deer again, but at a distance of some hundred yards. Hearing the growl, the bear drew her body half out of the bushes, remaining quietly on the lookout. Soon the deer again appeared, but his speed was much reduced, and as he approached the spot where the bear lay concealed, it was evident that the animal was calculating the distance with admirable precision. The panther, now expecting to seize his prey easily, followed about thirty yards behind, his eyes so intently fixed on the deer that he did not see the bear at all. Not so the bear; she was aware of the close proximity of her wicked enemy, and she cleared the briars before her and squared herself for action, when the deer with a powerful spring passed clear over her head and disappeared.

"At the moment the deer took the flying leap the panther was close upon him, and was just balancing himself for a spring, when he perceived, to his astonishment, that he was now face to face with a formidable adversary. Not in the least disposed to fly, he crouched, lashing his flanks with his long tail, while the bear, about five yards from him, remained like a statue, looking at the panther with her fierce, glaring eyes.

" They remained thus a minute : the panther agitated, and apparently undecided, and his sides heaving with exertion; the bear perfectly calm and motionless. Gradually the panther crawled backward until at the right distance for a spring ; then throwing all his weight upon his hinder parts to increase his power, he darted upon the bear like lighting and forced his claws into her back. The bear then, with irresistible force, seized the panther with her two fore paws, pressing it with the weight of her body and rolling over it. Carson said that he heard a heavy grunt, a plaintive howl, a crashing of bones, and the panther was dead.

" The cub of the bear came after a few minutes to learn what was going on, examined the victim, and strutted down the hill followed by its mother, who was apparently unhurt. The old trappers used to claim that it was a common practice of the deer, when chased by the panther, to lead him to the haunt of a bear; but I won't vouch for the truth of the statement.

"I have killed several of the creatures," continued Mr. Tucker, "but never had a very serious tussle, excepting once, up in what was then called the Klikatat Valley, in Washington Territory. I had been out after elk, but had not seen any, and was going up a very narrow, rocky ravine looking for their tracks. When I arrived at the head of the little cañon, I heard a snarl. Casting my eyes in the direction of the sound, I saw, to my dismay, a she panther on a flat ledge under a clump of dwarf cedars, with three kittens alongside of her.

"The enraged beast was in the attitude of springing, when I caught sight of her. I had no time to pull my rifle to my shoulder or jump aside. The ravine was so narrow that there was not room enough between the jagged walls to raise the piece and take aim. So quick were the cat's movements that she was almost upon me, her mouth wide open and her claws unsheathed ready for business. I was calm, for I had trained myself never to become excited under danger, and just as she jumped for me I cocked my piece, stuck the muzzle down her throat, and pulled the trigger as she fell upon my shoulder.

"The shot killed her instantly, but not before she had ripped some of the flesh off my arm as she rolled to the ground. It was a remarkably close shot, and a lucky one for me too. I skinned her, but was so sore that I had to return to my camp and dress my wounds, which healed in a few days."

When the story was finished, they all went to bed. Mr. Tucker promised the boys and girls he would remain over the next day and go on a rabbit hunt which they had planned for the morning.

It proved to be a glorious day as the sun rose next morning in a cloudless sky. Breakfast was out of the way by six o'clock, and the boys saddled their buffalo ponies, as they called those which they had captured out of the herd; their sisters' ponies also were saddled. Gertrude had a very gentle animal which her father had traded for with the Pawnees, but he was blind in one eye, and she called him Bartimæus, or Barty for short. He was hard to catch, but when caught was a quiet, easily ridden animal. Kate's was an iron-gray which had been born on a neighboring ranche, and especially broken for her benefit.

K

He was of that small breed peculiar to Texas.
and his power of endurance was phenomenal.
On a long journey, with only the wild grass to
subsist on, they soon wear out the pampered
steed of the stable.

The relation between Ginger and his young
mistress was remarkable for the confidence and
affection each had in and for the other.   He
was now five years old, and Kate had trained
him herself, but had never used whip, spur, or
severe curb during her long and patient training.
Consequently Ginger responded cheerfully and
promptly to her every command.   His education had been based upon gentleness and affection.   Her love for him was reciprocated in a
manner bordering upon human intelligence, thus
confirming the theory that kindness is more
effective in subordinating the brute creation
to our will than the club or kindred harsh
measures.

Kate's pony had never been confined by fence
or lariat; he roamed at will all over the beautiful
prairie or in the timber surrounding Errolstrath.
Yet day or night, in sunshine or in storm, if Kate
required his services, she had only to go and call

him, and if within the sound of her voice, he
would come galloping up to her, neighing cheerfully. When he arrived where she stood, bridle
in hand, waiting for him, he would affectionately
rub his nose on her arm or shoulder, and submis-
sively follow her to the house. If he happened
to be a long way off when she went to seek him,
she would jump on his bare back and ride him
home. He was always rewarded on these occasions with a lump of sugar or salt, of both of
which he was very fond. In the three years
of their companionship neither girl nor pony had
ever deceived each other: his sugar or salt was
never forgotten, nor had he once failed to respond
to her summons.

It made no difference when Kate wanted to
go anywhere, whether she mounted Ginger bare-
back and bridleless, or with saddle. Under either
condition she was perfectly at her ease, and he
equally obedient to her voice, by which alone
she frequently guided him.

He was as fleet as the wind, and more than
once Kate had run down a cottontail rabbit
in a spirited chase over the prairie.

She had christened him Ginger, not because

there was the slightest resemblance to that spice in his color, but rather for the "spice" in his nature.

Mr. Tucker rode his favorite large roan horse, which he had brought to the ranche with him, and which had carried him so bravely on the long and wearisome trip to the Elkhorn.

The happy little party left Errolstrath about seven o'clock, followed by the old hounds Bluey and Brutus, which were as anxious as their young masters for the excitement of the impending chase.

They rode down the Oxhide under the shade of the elms which fringed its border, until they arrived at the open prairie a mile from the ranche. There the dogs were ordered ahead, and began to run, eagerly looking out for a sight of any foolish rabbit, cottontail or jack, that might be out on the level stretch of country over which the hunters were now loping.

They had not gone on half a mile before they started a big jack from his lair of bunch-grass, where, probably, he had been taking a late nap. With a characteristic bound, jumping stiff-legged for a moment, he fairly flew over the short buffalo

sod, the dogs after him with every muscle strained
to overtake him before he could hide in some
tall weeds, or clump of plum bushes which were
scattered throughout the prairie at intervals of
five or six hundred yards.

Ever since they had come into possession
of their ponies, Joe and Rob had trained Bluey
and Brutus in such a manner that they scarcely
ever failed to secure any game they hunted.

The rabbit is a very swift creature, and has
a fashion, when pursued, of suddenly doubling
on his own tracks. Being so much smaller than
a hound, he can perform the feat a great deal
quicker than a dog, and if the latter is not
trained to know just what to do under such circumstances, and just how to run, the rabbit
almost invariably slips away from him. Bluey
and Brutus were taught not to keep close to each
other when on the run after rabbits. One of
them, generally the younger, when they first
started out for a hunt, remained far enough away
from his mate to make the turn when the rabbit
did, without forging ahead of him, as the fore-
most hound was sure to do, by the sheer momen-
tum of his rapid running. Then, the hound in

the rear had plenty of room and time to make the turn as soon as the rabbit, and was right upon him, as close as was the head dog when he doubled on his tracks. Then the old dog would recover himself and take his place behind the one that was now ahead, ready for the same tactics whenever the rabbit made another attempt to escape by again doubling on himself. So the race was conducted until the rabbit was caught. That was effected by the dog which happened to be ahead when he came near enough to thrust his long nose under the animal's belly and toss him high in the air, catching him in his mouth as he came down.

"Admirable!" said Mr. Tucker, as Bluey, who happened to be ahead, tossed the rabbit up and caught him as he fell toward the ground. "I tell you, boys, that's as fine a piece of work as I ever saw done by any hounds I have run with. You must have taken a great deal of pains to teach them to do their work so splendidly?"

"It took a long time," said Rob, who had really given more attention to training Bluey and Brutus, than had Joe, who had spent more of his spare hours in the camp of the Pawnees. "I sometimes almost gave up, they were so stupid when I first tried to teach them, but by degrees they understood what I wanted, and now I will put them against any hounds in the settlement for doing good work."

" I must admit," said Joe, " that all they can do is to the credit of Rob; he has more patience with animals than I have, though you know, Mr. Tucker, that I am never cruel. I know that you can accomplish more with a dumb brute by kindness than you can with a whip."

By noon the hounds had caught ten rabbits — six cottontails and four jacks — and, of course, were played out when the party turned back on the trail to Errolstrath. Here they found dinner waiting for them, and they all ate heartily, the delightful exercise having made them as ravenous as coyotes. The hounds were not forgotten; they had a rabbit each for their dinner, after eating which, they went to their accustomed beds on the shady side of a haystack near the corral, and slept all the rest of the afternoon.

Mr. Tucker left for his ranche about an hour after dinner, promising to come to visit the family again soon.

The family were worried about the impending Indian war, and when three o'clock had arrived his mother sent Joe up to Fort Harker to find out if there was any news of Custer and the troops under his command, who had gone after the Kiowas.

CHAPTER IX

INDIAN RAIDS — KATE IS MISSING — "BUFFALO BILL'S" OPINION — "BUFFALO BILL" FINDS HER LITTLE BASKET — THE SOLDIERS RETURN TO THE FORT WITHOUT FINDING HER — GRIEF OF THE FAMILY

IT was after dark when Joe returned from his mission to Fort Harker. He had been very kindly received by the officers, who had heard all about him from Colonel Keogh. The commanding officer told him that he wanted him to warn the settlers on the Oxhide that the war had really commenced; that General Sully had had a great fight on the Arkansas, and that it could not be considered as a victory. He told him also to tell the people on the creek that at any moment they might be visited by a hostile band, notwithstanding that they were in such close proximity to the post.

"You know yourself, my man, that the Indians have a faculty of going anywhere they want to go, and all the troops in the army might be fooled in regard to their movements. They are here to-day, murdering, and taking young girls captive, and a hundred miles away to-morrow.

"Tell the settlers," continued he, "that they must be on the lookout. I have not enough troops to put on guard on every creek. I wish I had; then there would be no danger of any sudden and unexpected raids. Why, do you know, Joe, that only yesterday, a band of Dog-soldiers made an attack on Wilson Creek, sixteen miles from here, and killed two men who were at work in their hayfield?

"It was reported to me about three hours after the affair had occurred, and I sent a company up there, but as they were only infantry, — I have no cavalry now at the post, — the Indians were soon out of reach.

"I want you to tell the settlers on the Oxhide to particularly watch their girls. The Indians will get some of them if they possibly can. They don't always murder them, but hold them in a terrible slavery in hopes of getting a heavy money ransom from the Government for their release."

Joe related to his parents all the conversation

he had with the officers at Fort Harker, and early the next morning he and his father rode through the settlement, warning the people to be on their guard.

Only ten days afterward, when the family at Errolstrath were just going to sit down to supper, it was discovered that Kate was missing. Gertrude went up to her room, supposing she might be reading there, for she was a great devourer of books, but she did not find her.

The boys hunted for her in all imaginable places on the ranche where they thought she might possibly be, but could not find her. When Joe and Rob returned from their fruitless quest, the family were too thoroughly frightened to think of eating. Mr. Thompson mounted his horse and started to make the rounds of the nearest neighbors to learn whether she was visiting any of them.

He returned to the ranche long after dark, but brought no news of her whereabouts, and found every member of the family in tears, and his wife nearly crazy. He was told that Kate's pony had come home, riderless, to the corral while he was absent, and a small sumac bush to which his reins were tied, had been torn up by the roots and was dragging at his feet. None of them could conjecture where she could be.

"My God!" exclaimed her mother, "if the Indians have captured her and carried her off, what shall we do?"

"Something must be done at once," said Mr. Thompson. "Joe, get your pony quickly, and we will hurry to the fort to learn whether any Indians have been seen or heard of in this vicinity to-day. If so, we will get the command-ing officer to send out a squad of soldiers imme-diately. You must go with them, Joe, and trail the savages if you can find any signs of them."

Joe and his father rode as rapidly to Fort Harker as their animals could carry them; went to the commanding officer's private quarters, as the business offices were closed after night, and reported to him the terrible anguish which the family were suffering.

They immediately adjourned to the Adjutant's office, and the commander sent his orderly for the officer of the day. When he made his appear-ance, he asked him whether any reports had been received concerning Indians being in the vicinity.

He replied that no such report had been received by him, and it was his belief that none of the hostile savages were in the immediate country.

At that moment, Buffalo Bill entered the room. He was chief of scouts at Fort Harker, and had just returned from some perilous mission to one of the military posts on the Arkansas, and was coming from the stable, to report to the Adjutant. He was told of the mysterious disappearance of Mr. Thompson's daughter Kate, and the opinion of the famous Indian fighter and courier was asked as to what he thought of the matter, as no Indians had been reported in the vicinity.

"Well," said Bill, "because you gentlemen have received no report of the savages, it does not follow that none have been here. *I know that they have been here, and to-day.* As I crossed Bluff Creek on my way here this afternoon, about six o'clock, I saw in the distance a band of Indians, numbering about ten or twelve, riding rapidly south. I hid myself in a ravine so that they should not discover me, but I got a good look at 'em with my field-glass. I think they were Comanches, though I can't be certain of that; they might have been Cheyennes or Kiowas;

they were too far off to be made out exactly.
Now, you ask for my opinion as to what has
become of the gentleman's daughter. I believe
those Indians have her; because they were riding so fast toward their villages, and they are,
you know, all south of the Canadian.

"But don't let Mr. Thompson worry too much;
the simple fact that she is a prisoner among them
is bad enough. If among the Kiowas, and the
chief, Kicking Bird, is in the village when the
band arrives with the girl, he will not allow her
to be harmed. He is a cunning old fellow, and
knows the value of money. He will have good
care taken of her, and get a heavy reward from
the Government for ransom. If she should fall
into the village of Sa-tan-ta, God help her! He
is the worst demon on the trail; but anyhow, I
don't think they will harm her, as they will want
a ransom."

"Well," said the officer, "I am sorry that I
have no cavalry at the post, but I will send a
detachment of the infantry after them in six-
mule wagons. I imagine it will be a useless task
to try to catch up with them if, as Buffalo Bill
says, they were going as fast as they could

to their village on the Canadian. Lieutenant
Hale," said he, turning to the Adjutant, "make
a detail at once of thirty men, and send them out
under a couple of non-commissioned officers on
the trail of the savages, if it can be found. Anyhow, some sign may be discovered that will tell
us whether the girl is with them."

Then turning to Joe, he said: "I wish that
you would go with the detachment, for you are
the best trailer in the whole country, not excepting our chief scout here, Buffalo Bill, and he's
the prince of all frontiersmen."

"Well," said Buffalo Bill, "I've just come off
a pretty hard trip, but I volunteer to go with the
party; if I can do anything in a case of this kind,
fatigue doesn't count."

"Thank you, Bill," said Mr. Thompson. "I will
return to Errolstrath and tell my family what has
been done, and your favorable opinion that the
savages won't harm her: that will be a comfort
at least. Good night, gentlemen," said he; and
he went out and untied his horse from the
hitching-post, and rode slowly home.

The night was quite dark, though there was a
little moonlight, but the detachment did not get

away from the post until long after midnight, as there was so much delay in hitching up the teams and turning out the soldiers who had gone to bed. By the time the little train of three wagons arrived at Bluff Creek, where Buffalo Bill had seen the Indians, the day was just breaking. They could not travel to that point from the fort very rapidly on account of the rough nature of the trail. It was nothing but a series of rocky hills after they had crossed the Smoky Hill, and was constantly becoming rougher as they approached Bluff Creek, which was well named on account of its high bluffs.

The party halted at the ford where they supposed the savages had crossed, and began to look for Indian signs. Pony tracks were plainly visible in the soft earth where the trail led down to the water, and Buffalo Bill dismounted and examined them carefully. He then asked Joe to get off his horse and count the hoof-marks. Joe did so, and both he and the famous scout agreed that there must have been about a dozen of the savages.

Crossing the creek, followed by the wagons, Joe and he ascended the hill on the other side.

They had not proceeded a quarter of a mile when Buffalo Bill picked up from the trail a small parflèche basket, which Joe immediately recognized as belonging to his sister.

"Look here, Mr. Cody, there is her name which I carved myself when I gave it to her. Now we know for a fact that the savages have captured her. I know why Ginger came home with that little sumac bush fastened to his bridle. Kate must have tied him to it, and when the Indians swooped down on her, the pony broke loose and tore up the little tree by the roots in his fright, for he was always scared out of his wits at the sight of an Indian."

The little detachment of soldiers rode on for a dozen more miles, when the mules showed unmistakable signs of fatigue. They could not be made to travel faster than a walk, notwithstanding the persuasive efforts of the blacksnakewhips in the hands of their drivers. So both Buffalo Bill and Joe reluctantly decided that it was no use to follow the Indians any farther. They knew the habits of the savages so well, that they were now probably a hundred miles ahead of them, for they always took loose stock

L

along with them so as to change animals when their own horses became leg-weary.

Very reluctantly, then, the cavalcade was turned round and headed for the fort, where the party arrived at about one o'clock. Buffalo Bill, as chief of scouts, reported the result of the trip to the commanding officer.

All were depressed at the failure of the expedition, but it was impossible that it should have turned out differently, and when Joe arrived at Errolstrath and related the story of the finding of Kate's basket, the grief of the family knew no bounds. All felt keen anguish at the absence of their favorite, and at her sad fate.

There was nothing to be done except to wait patiently for some action on the part of the Government in ransoming her if she was alive. The family settled themselves into a calm resignation, but the sun did not seem to shine so brightly, nor the birds to sing so sweetly as when the pet of the household was there. Even her antelope appeared to partake of the general gloom; it evidently missed its loving young mistress, and would wander around the house, disconsolately seeking her.

CHAPTER X

IMMEDIATELY after dinner on the day that Kate was missed, she bethought herself that the raspberries might be ripe. She wanted to surprise her mother and sister, but as will be seen, was surprised in such a manner that she never forgot it as long as she lived.

Without saying a word to her mother or Gertrude, she took out of her room a little basket made of par-flèche,[1] given to Joe by the Pawnees, and by him presented to her. She went out to the pasture, caught her pony, Ginger, saddled him, and rode out to the fatal raspberry patch where once she had such a terrible encounter with a she-wolf.

[1] Par-flèche is the tanned hide of the buffalo, without the hair. The Indians make baskets and boxes of it in which to pack their provisions and other articles when they move their villages.

It was a fortunate thing that both the girls had learned to ride, for a sad fate would have been in store for her had she not been a thorough horsewoman.

Arriving there in less than half an hour, she tied Ginger to a sumac bush, and to her delight found that the berries were quite ripe, and was soon absorbed in the task of filling her basket. Suddenly, with the rush of a tornado, and uttering the most diabolical yells, a dozen Comanches, dressed up in their war paint and eagle feathers, swooped down on the unsuspecting girl as a hawk swoops down on a chicken. Before she realized where she was, one of the red devils, leaning over from his pony, caught her by the arms and tossed her in front of his saddle, and in another instant the whole band was dashing away southward as fast as their little animals could be urged.

Of course, she fainted for a moment, but strangely held on to her basket. When she had recovered from her first shock, the Indians endeavored to make her understand by signs that they were not going to hurt her. In fact, they treated her with a sort of savage kindness. The great feather-bedecked brute made her as comfortable as he could in front of him, as he pounded the pony's flanks with his moccasined heels to urge it on as fast as possible.

They rode rapidly on, staying for nothing, crossed Bluff Creek, and reached the Arkansas River that night. They waited there for an hour to allow their ponies to graze, and themselves to eat and smoke. They rode on again until daylight the next morning, when the sand hills of the Beaver came in sight. There they halted for breakfast, and shared with the now relatively calm girl their dried buffalo meat, and bread made of ground-roots.

That evening they arrived at their village on the Canadian, more than two hundred and fifty miles from the Oxhide. Kate was turned over to the squaws, who treated her with the kindness innate in all women, because she was only a little girl. Had she been a young woman, that monster Jealousy, which makes his home even in the rude tepee of the savage, would have made her lot entirely different.

She was allotted to the lodge of an old squaw, the old chief White Wolf's fifth wife, whose duty

was to guard her and see that she did not attempt to escape. The savages, as Buffalo Bill
had suggested, simply wanted to keep her until
the Government should offer a ransom for the
little captive, so it behooved them not to abuse
her.

As the days rolled on in their weary length,
the white captive became more reconciled to her
fate. She had never given up the hope that the
officers at Fort Harker would soon send out the
troops to seek her, and that she would be restored
to her dear Errolstrath home and her parents.
At the same time, as she was a most excellent
horsewoman, she always thought that if the worst
came to the worst, she would make her escape
and again ride the long distance she had ridden
in coming to the village.

When she had regained her self-control on her
dreadful journey, she had looked around her and
had taken such observations as she could of the
lay of the country, the timber, and the general
aspect of the trail. Even then, in all the terrible
excitement of her capture, she thought of escaping at the first opportunity that offered itself.
She indelibly imprinted every tree, rock, and ford

on her mind, so that the long ride over the trail to the village was like a photograph on her brain, to be taken out of its storehouse whenever required.

In a very few days she had so ingratiated herself in the good opinion of the women of the village, that they really took a fancy to her. She willingly helped them in all the daily tasks heaped upon them by their hard masters. She learned readily how to tan the different furs which were brought into the place after a hunt, made moccasins, herded the ponies in her turn, and even became such an adept in cooking that she was soon permanently assigned as cook for the occupants of the tepee in which she was lodged. Then she was spared the dirtier and harder labor which fell to the lot of the Indian women, for she had been brought up by her excellent mother to perform all kinds of work in which a white woman is supposed to become proficient, and now it served her in a way that was never dreamed of.

The Indians occasionally had flour, but knew of but one way to prepare it. They made a kind of gruel, by boiling, and adding a little salt. A

most unpalatable dish! She made bread and
biscuit, which she baked in the most primitive
way, on a piece of thin iron before the coals of
the camp-fire; but then the food was so different
from that to which the savages had been accustomed, that no one was permitted to prepare the
meals for the lodge where she made her abode,
but the White Fawn, as they began to call her.

Like Constantinople, every village is overrun
with dogs, and they are the most vigilant guards
that can be imagined. No one may hope to
approach an Indian lodge, or a group of them,
without being saluted by a chorus of the most
unearthly barking and howling from the canine
cataract that is sure to pour out the moment a
strange footstep is heard. Kate, always a lover
of pets, immediately began to cultivate the friendship of the dogs of the village. There was, however, something more in her method than mere
natural affection for the brute creation; she had
an object in view. She knew that when the time
arrived for her to attempt to escape, the dogs
must be thoroughly attached to her, so that
they would regard any movement she might
make without the slightest suspicion. This she

oon effected, and in a short time every miserable cur in the village was her faithful ally.

The intense interest which she took in the herd of ponies may be imagined, for in one of them, at some time in the near future, was concentrated her hope of escaping from the hateful village. She had noticed a little roan pony which seemed to her to possess that power of endurance that would be so necessary when she started on her long and lonely journey to the beloved Oxhide. She knew that he was the swiftest animal of the hundred or more in the bunch, for she had watched him often when the dusky warrior who owned him rode away on the hunt. She had read in some favorite magazine at the ranche, that in the old tales of English minstrelsy, the roan horse was the favorite color of the heroes of those stories, and she selected that animal out of the herd to carry her away. So, whenever she could, surreptitiously, she petted him, and he became so attached to her that he would follow her like a dog.

The savages watched her very closely, and she dared not think of leaving the village for many long weeks. At last she appeared to be so

pleased with her new associations that their vigilance relaxed somewhat, and their eyes were not
always upon her.

She very rapidly learned the language of her
captors, and then, as she could talk to the women,
who were really kind to her, her isolation did not
seem so hard to bear.

The principal food of the savages was dried
buffalo meat, and, as it would keep sweet for
a long time and was very nourishing, she hid
portions of her rations in the hollow of an
old elm that stood near her tepee, for use on
the trip when the time arrived for her to run
away.

The clothes which Kate wore when she was
stolen soon began to show the hard service to
which they had been subjected, and finally she
had to resort to the blanket for a general wrap,
like her female associates. She had patched
her civilized dress until it was like Joseph's
coat, of many colors, but she tenaciously clung
to it, determining that she would wear it home,
if she was fortunate enough ever to return. So
she took it off and carefully stored it with her
buffalo meat in the hollow of the old elm.

She soon became aware that the savages were at war with the whites, for often when the warriors went away dressed up in their feathers and hideous paint, they came back with their ranks decimated, and then there was wailing and howling in the village.

She knew, also, that General Custer, whom the Indians called the Crawling Panther, was gradually outwitting them, for she heard the sobriquet they had given him often mentioned in their talks around the camp-fires.

CHAPTER XI

FIVE months had made their sad passage at Errolstrath ranche since Kate was carried off by the Indians. It was now November, and Thanksgiving, that day so sacred to every New Englander's heart, was rapidly approaching; it lacked but one week of its advent. Notwithstanding the sadness which still hovered over Errolstrath, the great healer, Time, had poured balm into the wounded hearts. There still remained the tender remembrance of the light which the absent one always brought into the house, and the parents still strove to fulfil their obligations to those who were left to them, so Thanksgiving was kept as it had been ever since the settlement of the family on the ranche.

The mince pies had been baked, the cider
bottled, and all that was lacking to make up
the complement of the great dinner was a turkey. As, however, the woods were full of them
around Errolstrath, no uneasiness was felt in
regard to the presence of the magnificent bird
when he was wanted.

Joe, upon whom the family depended to
keep the larder well supplied with game, intended to go and kill a wild turkey the next
day. Thanksgiving came the second day following on the twenty-fifth, so there was ample
time to procure the principal dish for the coming event.

Joe had long since ceased to hunt for mere
amusement. He had become a veritable pot-
hunter, not in the general sense in which the
word is used, that is, a man who only kills his
game on the ground, but he hunted only when
the family needed a change of diet, and desired
some kind of game.

It was Rob's duty that month to bring the
cows home and milk them, a duty at which
the boys took turn and turn about each month.
That evening he was returning home with his

charge, and was riding, as usual, one of the
buffalo ponies. As he was going along the
bank of the Oxhide, in the long grass which
grew in some places higher than a man's head,
his animal suddenly stumbled with both feet,
into a prairie dog's hole, and Rob was incon-
tinently thrown over his head, falling into the
long grass without receiving any injury. As
he started to his feet again, he felt something
struggling in his hands, for he had involuntarily
clutched at the ground when the pony so unceremoniously tumbled him off, and to his great
surprise, he discovered that he had accidentally
caught a large wild turkey! He held on to
the bird manfully, although it tried its hardest
to get away from him; and holding it by the
legs, he walked on to the corral and drove the
cows in. Then, still leading his pony, he arrived
at the house, and called his mother and Gertrude out, exclaiming: —

"I've got the turkey for Thanksgiving, and I
didn't have to shoot it, either!"

Joe, hearing the noise, came down from his
room, and learning what had caused the racket,
said: —

"By jolly, Rob, you are a lucky dog; but if any one read of the way you caught it, they wouldn't believe it. I never heard of such a thing before. I sha'n't have to hunt one to-morrow now, and I'm glad of it, for I want to go to the fort to try to find out how the Indian war is coming on."

"Well, Joe," said his mother, "as you needn't shoot one now, suppose you kill and pick it while Rob is milking, then hang it up some-where so that the lynxes can't get it, and in the morning Gertie and I will get it ready for the oven."

Joe then took it from Rob, who was still hold-ing the struggling creature by the legs, and taking it to the woodpile, he chopped off its head, then he picked it, and hung it up in the smoke-house as the safest place until his mother was ready for it in the morning.

Thanksgiving day opened clear and cool, but not at all cold, for November in Kansas is one of the most delightful months in the whole year. The Indian summer is then at its height, and the amber mist hangs in light clouds on every hill, giving to all objects a smoky hue. This mist rests particularly on the bluffs bordering that stream to which General John C. Fremont gave the name of " The Smoky Hill Fork of the Republican." He first saw it in the late autumn of 1843, when on his exploring expedition to the Rocky Mountains, and it is into that river that the Oxhide empties itself only a short distance from Errolstrath ranche.

It was intended to have dinner served promptly at noon, and Mrs. Thompson had so announced to her husband and children, who were all anxious for twelve o'clock to strike.

About ten, while she and Gertrude were busy in the kitchen, the boys out in the yard, and Mr. Thompson in the timber, marking some trees he planned to cut down, there rode up to the front porch a strange-looking figure on a roan pony which was evidently nearly blown in consequence of the pace at which it had been driven.

The strange object was seemingly a girl, but she was one mass of rags over which was thrown a red blanket, Indian fashion. Her hair was unkempt, and she sat crossways on her animal, like a savage.

Mrs. Thompson, hearing the sound of a horse's

hoofs on the buffalo sod in front of the house, went out with her dish-cloth in her hand to see who the intruder might be. Looking at her, she at first thought one of the Pawnee boys had come for Joe, but when she heard in a sad and apparently disappointed tone a voice which she could never have forgotten: "My heavens! mamma, don't you know me?" she recognized it as that of her lost daughter Kate. The cloth dropped from her hand, and she fell prone upon the porch, overcome by the shock.

Just as Gertrude, who had heard her mother's smothered groan, ran out with a tin dipper of water to dash into her face, Kate dismounted, and rushing to where her mother was lying, she threw her arms around her neck and began to sob violently.

It was then that Gertrude, for the first time, saw her sister Kate, and she, too, immediately fell upon her lovingly, and for some moments there was weeping, laughing, kissing, and hugging. The boys, in the back part of the house, and their father in the stable, hearing the voices, hurried to the veranda, and in another second all were kissing and hugging the ragged girl,

M

each one trying to outvie the other in their joy
at the return of the pet of the household.

They fairly dragged Kate into the sitting-room,
where, for a few minutes, they looked at her in a
dazed sort of way. Her mother was the first to
come to her senses.

"The first thing to do," she said, "is to get
some decent clothes on the child; then as soon
as Mr. Tucker comes we will have dinner. Oh!
my, what a Thanksgiving it will be!"

Kate was soon made comfortable in clean linen,
and a dress of her sister's, for she had outgrown
all that were of her own wardrobe five months
before.

At this moment Mr. Tucker rode up to the
door, and allowing Rob to take his horse to the
stable, the old man walked into the house. He
was the only invited guest on the Thanksgivings
at Errolstrath. All his family were long since
dead, and he was alone in the world; besides,
being a New Englander, he had not forgotten
how to appreciate the most important festival
of Yankee Land.

He was wonderfully taken aback when he saw
that Kate had returned, and he congratulated her

with his eyes full of tears; for he was a man with a warm heart, though his early life in the days of the old trappers had given him a rough looking exterior.

Kate looked like the dear Kate of old, as all sat down to a real Thanksgiving dinner. She was much browner than when she left Errolstrath, because of her constant outdoor life in the Indian village.

"Oh! Kate," said her mother, as the happy girl took her accustomed place at the table, between her father and Gertrude, "how earnestly I have prayed that you might be restored to us; I felt at times almost in despair, but the thought of the good God's promises to the patient, cheered me up, and I knew that in His own time my prayer would be answered. What a different Thanksgiving this is from what we all have expected, when we thought of Kate's vacant chair! Only think, we have never yet been separated on this blessed day during all the years we have lived at Errolstrath! But we little thought that we should be together to-day."

"We have much to be thankful for," said Mr.

Thompson; "excellent crops, good luck with our stock, and to cap the climax, our beloved Kate is restored to us."

The Thanksgiving dinners at Errolstrath were composed of those conventional dishes which make up the celebration of the festival in New England, and the one at Errolstrath that day was perfect in its resemblance to those of the old homestead in Vermont.

While they were discussing the good things on the table, Kate was told how Rob had got the turkey for the dinner, and also how matters had progressed at the ranche during her absence, for she was very anxious to know. Her father said that he had raised the largest crop of corn since he had been on the creek; that the wolves had carried off two calves from Errolstrath, but that many of the neighbors had suffered a great deal more from their depredations, and that a grand wolf hunt was contemplated by the whole neighborhood, for something had to be done to thin out the ravenous creatures. Gertrude told how many chickens she had, but Joe gave them all the best news they had heard for a long time.

" I was over at Fort Harker yesterday," he said,
"and I heard that General Custer had attacked
the camp of Black Kettle, the Cheyenne chief, on
the Washita in the Indian Territory, and completely wiped them out. The war is ended, and
the savages are suing for a peace which General
Sheridan says they will be sure to keep this time.
The commanding officer told me that Custer
would soon arrive at the fort, and that the settlers need have little more fear; that they may
go anywhere now without expecting to lose
their hair. He said that Sheridan had been promoted to the rank of lieutenant-general for the
brilliant success of his winter campaign, and that
he would shortly be at Fort Harker on his way
to Washington."

" Well, that is glorious news," said Mr. Tucker.
" No more stealing pretty little girls from their
homes, eh ? "

When Joe had finished his joyous piece of
intelligence, the family adjourned to the big sitting-room, and Kate was asked to tell the wonderful story of her capture and escape. She
seated herself in her favorite chair, an old Boston
rocker, brought from Vermont and nicely cush-

ioned at the back, and was making ready to begin, when her mother said : —

"What in the world, Kate, possessed you to go away from the house that day and to tell none of us where you intended to go?"

"Why," answered Kate, "I remembered that you were very fond of raspberries, and I thought that, as they must be ripe, I would saddle Ginger and go up to the patch to get some, for I wanted to surprise you. I took my little Indian basket —"

"Buffalo Bill found your basket on the trail the other side of Bluff Creek ford," interrupted Joe, "and that is how we came to know that the Indians had captured you."

"I remember now," said Kate, "that I held on to it for a long time and then dropped it. I don't know why I kept it in my hand. Well, as I was saying, I rode out to the patch, tied Ginger to a sumac bush, and began to pick the berries, which were ripe as I had expected. I had nearly filled my basket when with a dash that nearly frightened me out of my senses, a band of Indians came from the other side of the big ledge, and before I knew where I was, I

"I had nearly filled my basket."

found myself in front of a horrible-looking savage, and the whole band started south as tight as their ponies could go. I remember hearing Ginger give a snort, as he jerked up by the roots the bush I had tied him to, and fairly flew towards the ranche—"

"There, mother," said Joe, "that's just what I told you when Ginger came home with the sumac fastened to his bridle!"

"Oh, if I could only have jumped on Ginger's back," continued Kate, "before the Indians had got me, they never would have had the ghost of a chance of catching me. But they came upon me before I had the least idea they were anywhere near.

"We rode all that afternoon, halting for a few moments, long after dark, for the Indians to change ponies, as they had some loose ones with them. We kept on at a good gait all that night, until about daylight, when we stayed for more than an hour on the other side of the Arkansas River, to graze the ponies among the sand hills, and for the Indians to eat their breakfast. They were quite kind to me; gave me some dried buffalo meat, and brought me some

water from the stream in a horn, and tried to
make me understand that they did not intend
to harm me.

"Of course, I was frightened at the idea of being carried off by the horrid savages, but I tried
to keep my senses, and watched every tree and
rock on the trail. I looked at the sun to learn
which way we were going, and determined in
my mind that I would escape at the first
opportunity.

"On the tops of the highest points of the hills,
I saw the stone monuments, which Joe had often
told me were placed by the savages on their
travels from place to place, as marks to show
where water and wood are to be found."

"Yes," said Mr. Tucker; "you can see those
piles of stones on every hill about here; and from
them you can always see water or timber, indicating where to camp."

"They were to be seen on every divide we
crossed," continued Kate; "and besides, I saw lots
of the compass-plant, or rosin-weed, the leaves of
which, Joe had told me, always pointed north, so
I felt satisfied if I could ever escape, I would
have no trouble in finding my way back to the

Oxhide.[1]   After a long, wearisome ride, until the next morning, we arrived at the Canadian River, which the Indians called the ' Mai-om,' or Red, and on the bank of which was the village consisting of about a hundred lodges.

" There I was turned over to the women, who treated me very decently, and I immediately began to study the language, for I knew that that would help me in getting into their good graces. I willingly took hold of the work which falls to the lot of the squaws in every camp, and taught them how to cook after the white style. You may imagine I had plenty to do, for the warriors liked the biscuit I used to make, and they sometimes had a good deal of flour for which they had traded with the white men who bought their furs.

" I made friends of the dogs in the village, and there were hundreds of them, some of them miserable curs, but they could make more noise than a pack of wolves; and I thought if I could teach them to know me, they would not bother

---

[1] The compass-plant, or rosin-weed, as it is commonly called, is the *Silphium laciniatum* of the botanists.   It is found in luxuriance on every hill-top on the great plains, and resembles an immense oak leaf, which, while growing, always points its thin edges north and south, consequently broad surfaces east and west.

me when I attempted to run away ; for you know
that they are the most watchful animals imaginable.   At night, not the slightest sound escapes
their well-trained ears, and at the approach of a
human being, they set up the most terrific barking and howling you ever heard.   Well, I soon
made friends with every one of them, and I could
go around the village after dark, and they would
not utter a growl.

"I watched very closely the large herd of
ponies, — there were more than two hundred
belonging to the village, — to find out which
one of them was the fleetest, and had the most
endurance.   I picked out the little roan I rode
here, and, Joe, I will make him a present to you;
for if you had not taught me so much about
plants, and the methods of the Indians, and before all things else, taken such pains with me
when I wanted to ride a pony, I never should
have been able to run away and come home
safely."

"Thank you, Kate," said Joe.   "We have kept
Ginger just as finely as ever for you, and he is
the best pony in the whole country, I don't care
how many the Indians may have."

Kate went on with her wonderful experience. "Near the tepee where I slept I found an old elm tree that had a great hollow in it near the roots, and I determined to make it my store-house for the food I should need when I ran away. I did not, of course, begin to hide any-thing in it until I had been in the village for over four months. Then I used to save little by little of my portion of the dried buffalo meat, as I knew that it would keep for a long time without spoiling.

"We ate all sorts of things that at first rather disgusted me; puppy-stew, for instance. Now, mother and Gertrude, don't laugh; I really soon learned to like it, though I never expect to be compelled to eat it again. It is the cleanest thing the Indians have, if you will only get over the natural prejudice against eating dog. Why, just think, the puppies are only sucklings when they are eaten; they have tasted nothing but their mother's milk, and the mothers are fed on buffalo meat only.

"I suppose that you, mother and Gert, want to know how puppy-stew is prepared? Well, when the little things are rolling fat, as round as a ball of butter, the old woman who has charge of the lodge takes them up and feels them all over, and if satisfactory, she chokes them to death by literally hanging them to a tree with a buffalo sinew. When dead, they are singed before the fire, just as you singe a fowl; the entrails are taken out, and then the flesh is boiled in a pot, and eaten as hot as possible. The savages, particularly the old squaws, can take up in their buffalo-horn spoons, meat which would scald a white person to death, and swallow it without the slightest difficulty. I suppose that that, and their constant brooding over a smoky fire in the tepees, makes them look so old and wrinkled at an early age. They are the most horrid-looking witches you ever saw, and they would need no 'fixing up' to play the part in Macbeth."

"Talking of curious dishes eaten by the Indians," said Mr. Tucker, "up in Oregon, where I was trapping a good many years ago, the squaws make what I call Indian jelly-cake. They take the black crickets, roasted, which form a large portion of their subsistence, and make a kind of bread of them, after having ground them on a flat stone. They then spread on it the boiled berries of the service tree or bush, and if it was not manipulated by their very dirty hands, it would be very palatable."

"The Indians of the great plains," continued Kate, "live almost exclusively on meat; they gather a few berries sometimes, but their principal diet is buffalo meat.

"After I had been in the village for over four months, I began to think of trying to escape. My clothes were becoming more ragged every day, and I was obliged to resort to the blanket as a covering, though I kept what I had worn there as long as I could.

"One day there was a great feast in the village, with dancing and carousing, which the warriors kept up until long after midnight, and consequently slept very soundly. Now, thought I, is my time. So after I found out that the old squaw with whom I lodged was sound asleep, I crept up, and looked out to see what kind of a night it was. The moon was low down in the western heavens, but bright enough for me to see the trail, so I determined to make the attempt. I took a piece of buffalo robe for a saddle, and went out to the herd to catch the pony on which

I had had my eyes for such a long time, and had petted whenever I was not watched. The dogs, of course, had come out of their holes to see what was going on, having heard my almost noiseless footsteps; but recognizing me instantly, they did not set up their customary howl. They went back to sleep without making any trouble, and I walked out to the herd about a quarter of a mile away, and soon found the little roan I wanted. He came up to me without a neigh, luckily, and I fastened the piece of robe on him, tucked the dried buffalo meat, which I had taken from my hiding-place, into my bosom, and jumping on, started at a pace which, if I had not been a good rider, would have tossed me off before I had gone half a dozen yards.

"The pony seemed to know just what I required of him, for he ran on a good lope, with his belly almost touching the ground, and in a little while I had crossed the ford of the Canadian, and was going up the divide on the other side as fast as I dared to force him. I took a glance at the north star to get my bearings, for I dared not follow the broad trail, as the Indians would be sure to track me, and struck across the coun-

try, up one hill and down the other until day
began to break. Then I stayed a few seconds
at a small branch to let my pony drink and to
take a swallow myself, and on I went, not daring
to let him graze yet.

"Mile after mile the noble little fellow carried me until late that afternoon. Of course
I watered him at every creek I came to, but did
not halt until it had grown quite dark. Then
I took him about a mile down into a piece of
timber, unsaddled him and let him graze for
more than an hour. I kept my ears open, fearing every moment to hear the sound of ponies'
hoofs, for I felt confident that the Indians would
follow me the moment they discovered that I was
gone.

"When I thought he had sufficiently rested,
and I had eaten a small piece of the meat, I
mounted him again and started on a lope northward. I kept the little gallop, changing into
a brisk walk once in a while, until I could see by
the daylight the long silvery line of the Arkansas,
looking like a white snake in its many windings.
Then I felt pretty safe, after I had stopped and
watched the trail back as far as I could, which

was for more than two miles. I could see nothing like dust, nor hear a sound, so I began to hope that I had really escaped, and my heart began to feel lighter than it had for many a long month.

"I crossed the Arkansas, which the Indians call 'Mit-sun,' meaning Big, and it was up to my pony's breast, but he struggled through splendidly, though I got my moccasins wet, for the water came to my knees. I did not mind that, as I had often got wet through in the Canadian where we used to go swimming almost every morning while at the village. The squaws are very fond of the water in that way, but are not so clean with their hands as I would many a time have liked them to be.

"On the other side of the divide separating the Arkansas from the Smoky Hill, I halted in a box-elder grove to rest my roan, and rest myself, for I was nearly worn out. I felt very safe then, for I knew that I was approaching the settlements on Plum Creek, and if I had known, what Joe has just told us, that the war was over, I might have been at my ease all the way from the Arkansas.

"Early this morning I came to Bluff Creek, at the very spot where I had crossed with the Indians, and how my heart fluttered when I knew I was so near dear Errolstrath! From that creek I rode slowly, as I knew I had nothing to fear from the Indians, for the settlements were too thick, and besides it was daytime, when the Indians rarely attack.

"I often got off my pony when it grew too dark to see, to feel the leaves of the compass-plant, that I could always find without much hunting on every hill. Now, mamma and father, don't you think that I have made a famous ride?"

"We all think so," said her father; "it is one of the most remarkable on record, and we rejoice more than even you can imagine, to have our dear daughter back again, well as ever, after such an experience."

"Why don't the Indians raise corn?" inquired Rob, in a general way; "it is so easily grown out here on the plains."

"Some of the tribes do," replied Mr. Tucker. "The Sioux and the Mandans have always had their corn-fields, but as usual the women have to

N

do all the work. Do you know, Rob, that the
corn is a native plant of North and South
America, yet it has never been found wild?"

"Do tell us about it," said Mrs. Thompson;
and Kate asked if there were not some legend
connected with it, "for there is not a thing that
they eat, without its wonderful story."

"Certainly," replied Mr. Tucker. "There is a
beautiful legend among the Sioux, which I
learned from them when I was among them in
1840, and as it is not late yet, if you like, I will
tell it to you."

"Do! do!" all exclaimed in chorus.

"Of course," began Mr. Tucker, "among the
Indians the origin of corn is wrapped up in the
supernatural legends of the race, of which there
are several, differing materially, however, in their
details. Strange as it may seem, nowhere in all
the vast domain of both Americas, has a wild
species of corn been discovered; and yet the
inhabitants of these continents have used it from
the earliest times, of which even history has no
record. Yet, at some time in the unchronicled
past it must have grown wild. An unknown
benefactor of his race — one whose name not

even tradition preserves, excepting in unintelligible myths — saw somewhere, the feathery tassels and glossy blades with their silken ears amidst the foliage of a sedgy river bank, and owing to his first care, the wild plant, after many ages, has become the maize of commerce, and the king of all the cereals of the nineteenth century.

"When Columbus found the New World, corn was the staple food of all tribes of Indians from the far north to the extreme south, who attempted to cultivate the soil at all.

"The celebrated Père Marquette, the Catholic priest who passed his life among the savages, met with it at every point, on his memorable journey down the Mississippi River, in 1763. It has been exhumed from tombs of a greater antiquity than those of the Incas of Peru. Darwin discovered heads of it embedded in an ancient beach that had been upheaved eighty-five feet above the sea-level.

"That Indian corn is indigenous to America, has never been questioned by botanists, for Europe knew nothing of it until Columbus returned home from our shores.

"Longfellow has poetically told of one of the

Indian traditions of the origin of corn, in his
Hiawatha's Fasting.

"The legend was first transmitted to the white
men by Rattlesnake, and strange to say, he was a
chief of the Kansas or Kaw tribe of Indians.
He related it on an island at the mouth of the
Kansas River, in 1673, as is recorded in the old
French manuscript of an early traveller.

"It states that a band of a hundred Kansas
Indians in returning from a successful raid on the
Shawnees, of whom they had taken several prisoners, halted on the island, taking advantage of the
thick timber which grew in groups, as a conven-
ient spot to torture their captives.

"Père Marquette, whom the Indians called
'The White Prophet,' happened to be there most
opportunely; for through the respect and venera-
tion in which the monk was held, he saved the
lives of the hapless Shawnees, who were set at
liberty. That evening while eating their supper
of cooked hominy, the good priest asked for the
legend which told of the origin of Indian corn,
and Rattlesnake gave it, as he said he had often
heard it at his mother's knee.

"It is the same story the Sioux told me, but I

will follow the language of the old manuscript, for I have often read it.

"Once when the world was young, and there were but few red men in it, there was a chief whose wife bore him many children. Every summer added one and sometimes two to his family. They became so numerous that the father could not give them sufficient food, and the hungry children were continually crying. By great patience and skill in hunting, however, the chief at length raised a large family, until his eldest son reached the stature of manhood.

"In those days the red men all lived in peace and friendship. There was no war, and no scalp-locks hung from the doors of the lodges. The eldest son had the fear of the Great Spirit in his heart, and, like his father, he toiled patiently in the chase that he might assist in procuring food for his brothers and sisters.

"In those days all of the promising young men, at their entrance into manhood, had to separate themselves from the tribe, and retire into the forest, to see if the Great Spirit would grant them some request. During this time there was to be neither eating nor drinking, but they were

to spend the hours in thinking intently on the
request they were making of the Manitou.

"When the young man had gone a long distance in the forest, he began to pray to the
Great Spirit, and to ask for a favor which he had
long cherished in his heart for the occasion. He
had often felt how frequently the chase had disappointed the red men, and how often their
families had gone to sleep hungry, because they
had no meat. He had always determined when
his fasting and dreaming hour should come, that
he would ask the Great Spirit to give the red
men some article of food more certain than the
meat obtained in the chase.

"All that day the youth prayed, and thought
of his request, and neither water nor food entered
his mouth.

"At night, with a bright hope in his young
heart, he lay down to sleep. Soon he had a
vision. He saw a magnificently attired youth
coming toward him. He was clad in robes of
green, and green plumes hung gracefully about
his comely countenance.

"'My dear young friend,' said the stranger,
'the Great Spirit has heard your prayer, but the

boon you ask is a great boon; and you must pass through a heavy trial of suffering and patience before you will see the realization of your wish.

"'You must first try your strength with me, and suffer nothing to enter your lips until I am overcome, before you will receive your reward. Come, the night wears apace, let us wrestle amid the trees.'

"The chief's son had a big heart, and knew no fear, so he closed with his graceful antagonist. He found him endowed with muscles like the oak, and he had the wind of a wolf, that never was exhausted by effort. Long and long they wrestled, but so equal was their strength that neither could claim any decided advantage. 'Enough, my friend, for this time. You have struggled manfully. Still resist your appetite, give yourself up wholly to prayer and fasting, and you will receive the gratification of your desires. Farewell until to-morrow night, when I will return to wrestle with you again.' Then the young visitor, with his green plumes waving over his head, took his flight toward the skies, the green and yellow vestments with which he was clad expanding like wings.

"When the Indian awoke, he found himself panting like a stag when chased by the wolves, and the perspiration dropped from his body; yet his heart was light, for he knew a sign had come from the Manitou. Although he was very hungry that day, and some berries and grapes tempted him sorely, he refrained from touching them, resisting successfully these natural desires.

"Night came, and the young Indian closed his eyes in sleep; and lo! there was a continuance of his former vision. He saw coming toward him the graceful being he had seen on the previous night. The silken wings of green and gold swept through the air with great velocity, and the green plumes on his head waved rhythmically in their beauty.

"They again wrestled, as before, and although the Indian had neither eaten nor drunk, he felt his strength greater than in the previous conflict; and he obtained some signal advantage over his celestial competitor. They were struggling together when the morning commenced to look upon the world, and he of the green plumes thus addressed the Indian youth: —

"'My friend, on our next trial you will be
the victor. Now, listen how I instruct you to
take advantage of your conquest. When my
efforts cease I shall die. Strip me of my yellow garments and bury me in soft and new-
made earth. Visit my grave week by week,
for in a little time I shall return to life in the
form of a plant, which you will readily recog-
nize by its resemblance to me. Let no weeds
or grass be near me to keep the dew and sunshine from my green leaves, and once a month
draw the fresh earth to my body, that it may
grow and strengthen. When ears have shot
from my side, and the silk which shall fall from
their tops commences to dry, then pull the ear,
strip it of its garments as you will strip me
when I am dead. Place the milky grains before the fire which will cook the outside without destroying any of the juicy substance. Then
all the race of man will have a sweeter and
stronger food than they have ever known before. There shall be no more hunger upon the
earth excepting among those who have a lazy
spirit, or whom the Bad Manitou claims as his
own.'

"When the Indian awoke, he felt very weak from hunger, and it required all the resolution of which he was master to restrain the gratification of his appetite, but he passed the day in fasting and prayer, and at nightfall laid himself down to sleep.

"True to his promise, his friend of the green plumes again appeared in his trance, and again the wrestle commenced. The young Indian was exceedingly weak from his long fasting, but when engaged in the conflict he felt his heart grow big within him; his arms became as strong as the young oaks of the forest, and after a short struggle he threw his antagonist to the ground. The young Indian stood by the side of his adversary who said that he was dying, and told him to remember the instructions he had given him. The young Indian accordingly stripped the body of its vesture of mingled green and yellow, and carefully digging a grave, deposited it in the soft earth. He thought that the earth adhered to his hand in a strange manner, and at that moment he awoke, and found in his hand a seed such as he had never before seen.

"The Indian then knew that the Manitou had

heard his prayer, and that the grain was the body of his friend. He then went from the forest to the prairie, made soft the earth, and planted the strange seed sent to him in his dream.

"He then returned to his father's lodge, and the whole family were anxious to know if he had received any sign from the Great Spirit, but he evaded all inquiries and kept his important secret. Every morning, before the sun's bright rays had looked upon the earth, he was beside the grave of the seed, and carefully kept the grass and weeds away.

"On the morning of the ninth day, the faithful youth saw a green plant shooting from the earth, and as he gazed on its green blades, he knew at once the friend with whom he had wrestled.

"Once each month he drew the fresh earth to the stalks, which grew day by day until they far overtopped his own stature, and then there began to protrude from their sides the shoots from which a mass of silken fibres issued. In a short time the plant began to dry, as had been foretold to him, and then he invited his father, mother, brothers, and sisters to the spot and showed them what the Great Spirit had sent him at his fasting season. He then pulled one of the two ears and roasted it before the fire.

"The whole family tasted the new food, and they liked it. The other ear was kept for seed, and in a few years the red man had plenty of the new food which the Manitou had sent him."

"That is a beautiful story," said Mrs. Thompson, and the others all agreed with her. "Kate, you must be very tired; don't you want to go to bed and sleep like a Christian once more?"

"No," replied the young girl, "my muscles are 'like the oak trees in the forest,' as were those of the Indian who got the corn from the spirit with the green wings. Besides, it's only seven o'clock, and I want to look at you all for some time yet."

Before eight o'clock, Buffalo Bill and Colonel Keogh came over from the fort, as they had heard from some one from Oxhide that Kate had come home, and they wanted to see her.

They were both surprised at her excellent condition, and Bill ventured the remark that the Indians had certainly used her much better than they would have used him had he been in her place.

"I've no doubt of that," said Mr. Tucker; "they would have had a roasting frolic if they had caught you instead of our little friend Kate!"

"Well," said Colonel Keogh, "the war is ended, and I guess we have had the last trouble in Kansas that we shall ever have. The Indians are going peacefully to their reservations, where the Government will feed them, which is cheaper than fighting them, at anyrate! General Custer is at the fort, and he has heard so much of Joe that he wants to see him, and take him on a wolf hunt in a day or two."

"I'll go, Colonel, for sure, for they are carrying off calves and hogs every night from some of the ranches on this creek," said Joe.

"Talking about wolves," said Colonel Keogh, "I never saw so many together in all my life as I did after the battle of the Washita. We found the bunch of ponies belonging to the Indians, numbering about twelve hundred, and General Custer ordered them all to be killed, as a necessity, to prevent other savages from getting them. A Plains Indian without a horse to ride is as helpless as a child. He won't walk, and it was thought that by killing all the ponies we found, it

would cripple the savages as effectually as if we
killed the same number of warriors. The bunch
was driven into a narrow cañon near their camp,
and as they huddled against the high rocky wall,
a detachment of the cavalry was detailed to shoot
them. We camped near there for a few days,
and at night the wolves would congregate there
to feed upon the dead bodies of the ponies. I
suppose they came from a distance of a hundred
miles, for you know a wolf thinks nothing of
going that far for a good meal. It happened to
be the time of the full moon, and just after nightfall a lot of us used to go and ride on top of the
bluff to watch the wolves come to the feast. I
think it is no exaggeration to say that five thousand of the hungry creatures gathered there
every evening, as long as any flesh remained on
the bones of the slaughtered ponies. Such snapping, snarling, growling, and fighting was never
heard before. You could hear them for two miles
easily. Some of them were so pugnacious and
ravenous that they actually killed and devoured
each other! I do not believe such a scene was
ever witnessed before or will be again."

"You have all heard that Sheridan has been

promoted to be lieutenant-general, and Sherman to be general, as Grant has been elected to the Presidency?" said Buffalo Bill. "Sheridan received notice on Kansas soil of his well-deserved promotion, and it makes the place classic ground. I will tell you how it was. Of course, official notice of the promotion was daily expected, as it had been seen in the papers from Washington, but the mails were very irregular in the vast uninhabited region south of the Arkansas. It was carried by the scouts from Fort Hays, the nearest railroad point, and they also took despatches to the scattered military posts that had been established temporarily, in the form of camps, cantonments, or wherever a detachment of troops happened to be. Early one morning General Sheridan, accompanied by two officers of his personal staff, left Camp Supply in the Indian Territory for Fort Hays, to take the railroad for Washington, where he had been ordered to report. When the party had arrived at the foot of a high mountain, just on the border of this state, they saw far ahead of them on the trail made by the troops in going into the field, a dark object moving rapidly toward them. As the dis-

tance between them lessened, they noticed that
it was a horseman whose animal, flecked with
foam, and with distended nostrils, was straining
every muscle to reach the ambulance. In a few
moments the sound of the horse's hoofs were dis-
tinctly heard on the hard trail, and when he had
approached near enough, its rider, the excited
scout, recognized Sheridan among the occupants
of the ambulance. He rose in his stirrups and
waved his hat in one hand, while in the other
he held up a piece of yellow paper, crying out
at the top of his voice: —

"'Hurrah for the lieutenant-general!' The
paper he handed to Sheridan was a telegram from
the President, informing him of his promotion."

"Well," said Colonel Keogh, looking at the
old-fashioned clock in the corner of the room,
"I had no idea it was so late. It's nearly ten.
Come, Cody; we must get back to the fort."
Then saying good-night to all, with an admoni-
tion to Joe not to forget the wolf hunt, of which
he said he would send him word, they mounted
their horses and rode off.

Mr. Tucker was to remain until morning, so
they all retired, after having passed one of the
most cheerful Thanksgivings in their lives.

CHAPTER XII

THE allied tribes of the plains, now thoroughly whipped into subjection by the gallant Sheridan and his intrepid subordinates, Custer and Sully, went sullenly to the reservations recently established by the Government in the Indian Territory, and "white-winged Peace" once more spread her pinions over the fair land of Kansas. The settlers could go from one village to another with perfect immunity from sudden attacks by savages hidden in some ambush on the trails, so the state made phenomenal strides toward a greater civilization.

Crops were enormous in their results when the virgin soil was turned to the sun, but the wolves, especially in the vicinity of Errolstrath, seemed to increase with the prodigality of Jonah's gourd. They became so persistent in their nightly dep-

redations at the ranches, that only by a concentrated effort of the neighborhood to exterminate
them could stock-raising be made profitable.

A few days after Colonel Keogh's visit to
Errolstrath on that happy Thanksgiving when
Kate had come back safely to her home, an orderly from Fort Harker dismounted in front of
the house, bearing a note to Joe from General
Custer. It stated that the General proposed to
hunt the wolves the day after to-morrow, and
desired him to invite Mr. Tucker, the old trapper,
and as many more of the neighbors who were
good shots, as would like to go. He wanted the
party to meet him at the mouth of the Oxhide
as early as seven o'clock. From this point he
intended to go to the general rendezvous of the
beasts in the limestone region, down the Smoky
Hill.

As soon as dinner was over at Errolstrath, Joe
saddled his pony, and started for Mr. Tucker's
ranche three miles away, to invite him to come
over to stay all night and join Custer and the
others of the party on the morning of the hunt.

Rob was at the same time told by his father to
get his pony and deliver General Custer's invita-

tion to as many of the neighbors as he could reach, and return by sundown. He left promptly on his mission, but went in a direction exactly opposite from that of his brother.

When he had loped along about a mile up the Oxhide, his attention was attracted by a curious noise which seemed to come from the bank of the stream. He rode his pony through the brush toward the strange sound, and what was his surprise to see two snakes fighting right on the extreme edge of the water where the bank was only just above its level. One of the reptiles was a black water-snake, and the other a bull-snake nearly twice as thick round as his opponent, but not quite as long. The bull-snake had his tail firmly wrapped around a sunflower stalk, and the other had his attached to a big weed. Each had hold of the other by the middle and was trying to pull in an opposite direction. It was evidently the intention of the black snake to drag his antagonist into the water and drown him, for he is a good swimmer, while the bull is not, and the latter was just as determined that his enemy should not get him into the stream.

They were both stretched to their utmost tension, and as Rob said, when he told about them on his return, he expected every moment to see them break in two; for both were drawn out as thin as a clothes-line. At last the hold of the bull-snake gave way, and the impetus, like the snapping of a whip, threw them both into the water. Now the black snake had a decided advantage, for he was in his element, and he immediately exerted every muscle to draw his antagonist's head under. Finally, after a severe struggle he succeeded in holding him there for a few moments, and when he let go, the bull-snake's dead body rose to the surface. Then the black snake gave a few shakes to his tail and darted off under the water, apparently not the least injured by his death-struggle with his larger antagonist.

Both boys returned to Errolstrath before sundown, and as it was Rob's month to take care of the cows and milk them, he went promptly about his business. Joe, after taking Mr. Tucker's horse to the stable, and feeding the other stock, returned to the house, and sat in the big room, talking to his guest for half an hour, until supper was announced.

Supper being cleared away, all adjourned to the sitting-room again, and the boys and girls proposed that the old trapper should relate some more of his experiences in the Rocky Mountains, when he was a young man; a request with which he cheerfully complied whenever he passed a night at Errolstrath.

After all were comfortably seated in their accustomed places, Rob told of his adventure with the two snakes on the bank of the Oxhide, when Joe, after his brother had finished, remarking that coincidences were curious, stated that he, too, that same afternoon, had had an adventure with three snakes — one more than Rob.

"When I reached the broad military road to Fort Sill," said he, "at the crossing of Mud Creek, I noticed some distance down the trail a terrible commotion. The dust was flying as if it had been twisted around by a whirlwind, and by looking steadily I could see something moving on the bare earth, where the grass is all worn off the road. I rode slowly up to the moving object, ready for any emergency, when I discovered three bull-snakes, two of them of immense size, the third one not so large. They had a half-grown cottontail among them, and were fighting bravely for the sole possession of the little creature, which was already nearly dead. I thought I would stay to see the fun, so I whipped the smaller one, and one of the larger of the reptiles away. They went hissing into the grass, as I applied my riding-whip to them pretty lively. Then I sat still on my pony to watch the single snake enjoy the meal I had so opportunely provided for him.

"Presently he began to wind his long body around the rabbit, and I could hear the bones of the poor thing crack as the muscular pressure was applied. He then gradually unfolded himself, turned his head toward the muzzle of his prey, dislocated his jaws, and commenced to take in the rabbit.

"Little by little the rabbit, which was much larger than the snake's body, disappeared, until it was entirely enveloped by the reptile. Then he coolly reset his jaws, and after a series of hisses — perhaps he was thanking me for my kindness in interfering on his behalf — he crawled away into the thick grass. I let him go, Mr. Tucker; for we never kill a bull-snake, they are

such good hunters for gophers, mice, and even
rabbits, which are becoming such a nuisance
here. I saw several wolves, of course; you can't
go a mile anywhere without seeing them, but as
I carried no gun with me I did not try to inter-
view any of them."

" I expect to have a good time the day after to-
morrow," said the old trapper, "and it will recall
some of my own experiences with them years ago."

"Oh, do tell us about it!" said Kate; " I just
love hunting adventures."

"All right, Kate; you have grown into a kind
of savage since your life with the Indians, eh?"

" I heard lots of wonderful stories from the
warriors when they sat around the fire at night,
but they told such abominable yarns that I didn't
believe them. They can stretch a thing pretty
well, I tell you," answered Kate.

"Begin, please, Mr. Tucker," said Rob, who
was as interested as any of the family.

" Well, then," said he, " I will tell you of the
brave deed of a Mexican, which occurred a good
many years ago, when I was down in Southern
California.

" He was a native, and named Amador Sanchez, well known in the Sierra Nevadas as a brave and successful hunter. He had a terrible fight with one of those great shaggy, gray mountain wolves. The struggle lasted for several hours, and ended by both combatants being laid prostrate on the ground. They were so completely exhausted as to be unable to reach each other from want of sheer physical strength. In that condition they passed one whole night. On the following morning, when the Mexican had recovered sufficiently to be able to creep to his shaggy antagonist, he found him dead.

"The terrible conflict grew out of the Mexican's daring attempt to save the life of a boy who was about to be torn to pieces when the Mexican attacked the wolf.

"At one time the wolf had the youth under him in such a way that it was impossible for Sanchez to plant a ball in any vital organ without imperilling the boy's life. Nothing daunted, however, with both revolver and rifle, he succeeded in lodging several bullets in other parts of the savage beast. Still the enraged brute clung to the unfortunate child, using every endeavor to tear him to pieces and horribly mangling every part of his body. At this juncture, the brave Mexican hunter could no longer refrain from active effort. He dropped his pistols and rifle, drew his sheath-knife and slung-shot; then winding his blanket around his left arm to protect it, he rushed in and compelled the animal to turn upon him, and so gave the boy a chance to escape.

"Wounds were freely given and returned, but the wary Sanchez fought with much dexterity and determination. The wolf finally became so mad with rage and pain, that he closed in upon the Mexican and threw him headlong upon the ground, where he remained almost senseless for a few moments before recovering his breath.

" Instead of following up his advantage, the beast, doubtless believing his enemy dead, because he did not move, commenced to examine and lick his own bleeding wounds. The spirit of the intrepid Mexican, however, was up, and he determined to conquer the wolf or die.

" Early in the struggle, by a blow from his slung-shot, Sanchez had succeeded in breaking the brute's lower jaw, and that was unquestionably the fortunate wound which eventually gave the victory to the Mexican.

" Sanchez renewed the fight as soon as he felt himself sufficiently rested, and, by adopting some curious tactics, in which he was materially assisted by a clump of trees, he succeeded in putting some heavy blows with his knife right into its vitals. At this, the wolf was aroused again to an unendurable madness, and, gathering himself for one grand effort, he bit at the Mexican's head and once more felled him to the earth. From this final attack, and his previous loss of blood, the brave man fainted dead away. How long he remained in that state he could not tell; but when he became conscious again, he found that the victory was on his side, for the wolf had breathed his last.

" The poor boy, as soon as the battle was decided, as he supposed at the cost of his friend's life, started for the village, arriving there late the following afternoon. Upon hearing his story, a party of well-armed men immediately went to the scene of the struggle, to bury their brave comrade. They were guided by the boy, who was able to ride a pony

" Arriving at the spot about midnight, they found Sanchez in a most pitiful condition. His flesh was terribly mangled, his clothes were torn to ribbons, and his back and shoulders were one mass of lacerated wounds, inflicted by the sharp teeth and claws of the wolf.

" Although he received the most delicate care and assistance at the hospital from those noble women, the Sisters of Charity, it was many weeks before he was able to resume his occupation of hunting. Even then he owed his life to his wonderful recuperative powers and his iron constitution."

" What a terrible time he must have had," said Kate. " The gray wolf is an awful animal to be attacked by. Do you know that they very frequently go mad, and then many savages are bitten, and die a horrible death from hydrophobia? One of the warriors was bitten while I was down in the Indian village. He had a hand-to-hand tussle with the wolf, and although he was only slightly bitten, he died raving."

" Yes, they are bad brutes to deal with," said the old trapper, "particularly those huge fellows that hunt in packs; a man has not the

slightest chance with them. I know that in
Oregon, about twelve years ago, the mail rider
for the military posts of Forts Dallas and
Simcoe was caught in the mountains by a
pack of them, and nothing of him or his animal was found excepting the letter sack, the
hoofs of his horse, and some buttons, with other
portions of the rider's clothing."

"Have you ever had a personal encounter
with any of the terrible beasts?" inquired Mrs.
Thompson.

"Oh, yes!" replied the old man. "I'll tell
you all about it."

"In 1856, I tried to ranche it in the central
portion of Washington Territory. I had no
neighbor nearer than thirty miles. I was a
little lonesome at first, because it was really
the first time I had been without partners, and
I saw my neighbors but once in a whole year.

"I remember that I started to visit John
Elliott. I felt that I needed company, and he
and I had trapped together some years before,
and were well acquainted.

"Towards evening, I started for my thirty-
mile walk. It was in December, and of course,

cool, with a magnificent full moon to light my trail through the deep forest and over the prairie.

"I had gone about two miles, I think, and as I neared a small lake, and was tramping along the edge of the water with my rifle carelessly swinging in my left hand, I suddenly heard a growl that startled me, and stopping at once, I saw a great wolf standing with his paw buried in the carcass of a red deer, and his mouth full of its flesh. The brute was not chewing, for his jaws were motionless, and he looked at me as if deciding which was the better meal for him, that which he had under his feet, or I. He was an immense animal. I don't think I have ever seen a larger wolf. If I had left him alone and gone about my business, he would not have troubled me. They are generally cowards, and will run at the sight of man, unless provoked or cornered, or are running in packs, when they will fight to the death.

"I, like the fool that I was, raised my rifle, took a quick aim at him, and pulled the trigger. He jumped at the instant I fired, and although I aimed at his heart, I missed it and hit him in the upper part of the fore leg.

Then with his mouth wide open, showing his
white teeth, and the froth running down the
sides of his cheeks in his rage, he came for
me with a howl, which I thought was answered
by about fifty more in the timber.

"It didn't take me ten seconds to get up
into the fork of an oak tree which stood only
a few feet away. By the time I was safely settled in my seat, there were four more of the
great grizzled beasts right under me, smacking
their chops and whining as if their mouths
watered for a taste of my flesh. If I could
have talked to them in their own way, I would
have suggested that they go and feast off of
the deer which still lay intact.

"Then, as I could not make them go away by
mere suggestions, I loaded my rifle and shot one
of them as dead as the deer. That made more
food for the others, as they will eat each other
under certain circumstances, but that particular
time was not one of them. I didn't blame them,
for the brute I had killed was a long, gaunt,
miserably thin, mangy-looking creature that
seemed as if he had not had anything to eat
for a month.

"The refuge I had sought from the ravenous beasts was but a sapling, and I expected it every moment to break with my weight. Presently, I heard the crotch begin to split, and letting my rifle drop, I was quick enough to catch my arms and legs around the trunk of the tree, and hold on for life until I could draw my knife and shove it into my belt ready for use.

"Having accomplished this, I watched my chance, and if there ever was such a scared wolf as the one round whose back I wound my arms when I fell, I'd like to see him!

"We rolled on the ground together, and the other three just backed off to watch the fight, and a pretty moonlight tussle it was. He got my body under him at last, and I thought I was done for.

"I felt a little faint when he sunk his teeth into me, but he didn't seem to like the hold he had, so he pulled his teeth out of me, tore my coat, shirt, and flesh, then seized my fur cap and shook it for a moment, which was a lucky mistake for me on his part. I felt his wet lips on my forehead, and had just time to let go my hold on his throat and clutch my knife, when he seized

my cap again and made an attempt to swallow it.
His throat was in no condition to get it down,
however, for my knife-blade was through his
jugular, and the point of it in his spinal marrow,
and in another minute he was dead wolf!

"I bled considerably when I got up, but I
wasn't weakened a bit. The whole affair had
occurred in half a minute, and I was ready for
the other three, who now all attacked me together. I caught up my rifle and struck one of
them across the nose and floored him. As he
picked himself up I seized him by the hind foot
and fell upon him. If the first wolf was frightened when I tumbled on him from the tree,
this one was more so. I can never forget the
awful howl he gave as I stood up on my feet
again, and swinging him into the air, struck one
of the remaining two a terrible blow with his
body.

"The first one I had wounded was scared at
the novel fight, and tucking his tail between his
legs, vanished into the woods, and I was left with
only two on my hands. I caught up one of them
as I had caught the other, and his comrade took
to his heels and was soon out of sight.

"I stood up on my feet again, and swinging him into the air,
struck one of the remaining two."

"The one I held by the heels, I swung twice around my head and then let him fly. The centrifugal force, as they used to call it at college, forced out his wind, and his scream, as he shot through the air, was diabolical. He went fully a rod into the water, and his howl only stopped when he struck it. I was weak and faint now from the tremendous exertion. The beast came up again, and struck out for the shore. When he reached it, he did not dare to approach me, but stood there as if petrified.

"At last he began to move off. I followed him slowly, and saw that he was getting tired. Presently he stopped again and tried to climb on the top of a shelving rock, but he was very weak, and just as he was making the attempt a second time, I raised my rifle and sent a bullet into his heart.

"I was now rid of all my foes, but too weak to walk much further, so I went back to my cabin and gave up my proposed visit until I was recovered from my wounds."

"Well," said Joe, "that beats my fight with the panther. We sha'n't have any such trouble on the day after to-morrow, though, for we shall

P

have a big enough party to fight a whole mountain full of them."

It was long after ten o'clock when Mr. Tucker had finished the thrilling story of his fight, and then the family all retired — some of them to dream of wolves, bears, and panthers perhaps.

CHAPTER XIII

THE morning of the wolf hunt came at last. Before six o'clock, Mr. Tucker, four near neighbors, and the two Thompson boys rode out from Errolstrath toward the appointed rendezvous, at the mouth of the Oxhide.

As all dogs work better on an empty stomach, the hounds, Brutus and Bluey, had not been fed that morning, so that their appetites for the chase should be keen.

The little party from the ranche arrived at the mouth of the Oxhide before the contingent from Fort Harker. They did not have to wait many minutes, for they soon saw a cloud of dust on the Smoky Hill trail, and presently the General's four great hounds came bounding along. Closely following them was Custer on a magnificent animal. Colonel Keogh rode his favorite horse,

Comanche, which had been wounded in the battle with the Cheyennes, on Mulberry Creek, when the command had a doubtful victory under General Sully. Comanche was destined to become more celebrated a few years later, when he and a single Crow Indian were the sole survivors of the unequal fight with the Sioux under the notorious Sitting Bull. It was there that Custer and all of the famous troopers with him went down to annihilation, in the valley of the Rosebud.

The General and Colonel Keogh greeted the party, and they rode on at a slow pace. They wanted to save the wind of both the horses and dogs, for the supreme moment when the wolves should give them all the excitement they might desire.

About seven miles from Errolstrath, the Smoky Hill makes a grand sweep to the southeast, the curve forming nearly half a circle. Bordering the river at that point is a series of immense limestone bluffs whose scarped sides come down to the water. The plateau which crowns the bluffs is honeycombed with holes, the dens of the big prairie wolf. They intended literally to beard the ferocious beasts there, for the wolf prowls by night and remains in his lair in the daytime. The General, the Colonel, the old trapper, and the boys were in front, while the hounds trailed after the horses, and were not allowed to advance until the word was given for them to do so.

Custer's dogs were of rare breed, and had been presented to him by some English or Scotch nobleman. They were rough in coat, muscular, fleet of foot, and fully able to cope with the biggest wolf that dared tackle them.

The zigzag trail leading to the summit of the high bluff where the business was expected to begin, was reached about half-past seven, and the tedious ascent was commenced. Arriving on the top at a point where a heavy belt of timber skirted the edge toward the river, they all halted to rest a few moments before they went out into the open where the wolves were.

An occasional low growl and a snarl were wafted by the breeze toward them, where they were concealed among the great trees. The hounds listened with ears cocked up, and uttered a whine now and then, as they gazed wistfully into their masters' faces. They were impatient for the fray like the charger who "smelleth the battle afar," but the time had not yet come for them to do their work.

The morning was deliciously cool. The ground was just covered with a slight coating of frost, making friction enough to insure safety for the horses. They would be called upon to do some hard running, and the rough plain where the wolves were, was sandy and treacherous, from the constant digging and scratching of the quarrelsome beasts themselves.

"A perfect day for the fun," said the General, turning to the old trapper, who had dismounted and was cinching his saddle a little tighter.

"Yes, General," replied he, "we could not have a better morning. The wind is just right for the dogs' noses, though I suppose those beautiful hounds of yours run both by scent and sight?"

"They are fine specimens of their species, not very graceful or beautiful, perhaps, but for muscle and endurance, I don't believe that there is a wolf on the plains which can get the better of one of them in a fair fight. They have had several tussles single-handed, but so far have come out without anything more serious than a few scratches. Their jaws are as powerful as a bull dog's, and they hold on with all that animal's tenacity. I look for some fine sport to-day; there will be some lively coursing if we succeed in getting the wolves out of their holes."

"Bluey," said Joe, who was sitting on his pony alongside of Custer, "is a great fighter; he has had three or four tussles with wolves, and came out on top every time. He has the most wonderful shaking powers I ever saw in any dog, and he has whipped two or three bull dogs in the neighborhood. They all give him a wide berth now, whenever they see him coming. Brutus is quite a young hound yet, and although he is good with rabbits, and did some splendid work when we had that fight with the lynx, he has never really shown what he can do. I guess he'll have a chance to show his mettle to-day."

"I advise all of you to cinch up your saddles," suggested the General, "as Mr. Tucker has already done, for you don't want to be tumbled off by a loose cinch. We'll make a break for the wolves in a few minutes; the hounds are uneasy, and I guess our horses are sufficiently rested now."

When the last saddle was cinched up, Custer
gave the word "forward," and the party moved
out of the timber.   The hounds cavorted around
when they saw signs of active work, but they
were restrained from rushing too far ahead by
a word from their masters.

The hunters rode slowly at first, until they had
emerged from the timber.   They then broke into
a lope, separating to a distance of about fifty
yards from each other.   Custer was on the right,
followed by the old trapper and Joe; while Rob
and Colonel Keogh with the others of the party
brought up the left.

Although they were out of the standing timber, there were a great many fallen trees scattered
over the ground, and they were obliged to jump
over these, as they could not afford to waste the
time to go round.

There was one immense black walnut trunk
over which all had gone very easily excepting
Colonel Keogh and Rob.   When these two
reached the obstacle, Rob's buffalo pony took
it flying, but as Comanche rose to make the leap,
the effort burst the cinch of the saddle, and the
Colonel was thrown.   He fortunately struck on

his feet and held on to the bridle reins, so the animal did not get away. His orderly rushed up, and it did not take more than five minutes to change saddles, and give the Colonel a mount again.

By that time Custer and the others were far in advance, for they had increased their pace as the hounds sighted their quarry. Some were in full cry, the rest silent, according to the habits of their species. A huge wolf had come out of his hole to learn what the thud of the horses' hoofs meant, had seen the dogs, and immediately bristled up ready for battle.

The lean and hungry-looking brute stood motionless, awaiting the arrival of the pack of hounds. The hair along his spine stood erect like a mad cat's, and his tail swelled to twice its normal proportions. They were heading for him with tongues out and their long necks stretched, ready for the impending battle.

In another instant, when the shock came, there was a chaotic whirlwind of wolf, dog, hair, and blood, accompanied by snarls, growls, and squeals. This cyclone of enraged canines was enveloped in a cloud of dust which fairly obscured the combatants for a few seconds; but when it settled there was a dead wolf, literally torn to shreds, and a hound or two limping along, nearly *hors de combat*, after the terrible struggle.

The noise of the fight caused a dozen or more of the denizens of the bluff to crawl out of their dens and look around to learn what was meant by this invasion of their sacred precincts.

Some just poked their heads up, and all you could see were their great ears. Others came up bristling with fight, and some, the cowardly ones, giving one look at the party of horsemen and the pack of hounds, tucked their bushy tails between their legs, and scooted off over the plateau, yelping like whipped curs!

In a moment, spying those wolves that had apparently accepted the wager of battle, the dogs made a grand rush for them, some in pairs, some singly.

General Sheridan owned a magnificent smooth-haired hound, named Cinch, from the fact that round his belly was a dark circle, resembling a saddle-cinch. He was a very powerful animal, and had been brought with the pack by General Custer, on account of his well-known staying qualities. Cinch had selected a monstrous beast, a little larger than himself, as his victim, and forthwith attacked him singly.

The wolf stood firmly at the mouth of his den, awaiting the approach of Cinch with a sort of self-satisfied look, as though he would tear to pieces that civilized specimen of his own genus. With a growl and a snapping of their great white teeth they came together. How the hair did fly as they bit whole mouthfuls out of each other! It was an awful struggle for canine supremacy. Every one of the party abandoned his quarry elsewhere — although Bluey was making a glorious fight with another monster not a hundred yards away, and the rest of the pack were hard at work on a number that had attacked them in concert — to witness the battle royal between Cinch and the largest wolf that they had ever seen.

At last Cinch succeeded in getting a firm hold on his shaggy antagonist's throat. It proved to be a "knock-out," for when Cinch had done with him, the wolf was stretched out dead. The hound himself did not escape without serious wounds. His fore paws were bitten through and through. One of his eyes was badly torn, and great pieces of hide hung in strings from several parts of his body. He was nearly done for, so badly hurt, that the General told one of his orderlies to take the poor dog on the saddle in front of him, and carry him back to the fort for repairs.

They then turned their attention to Bluey. By the time they came up to him he had just finished his antagonist as completely as had Cinch. The wolf was dead, and the old hound was busy licking his own wounds, of which he had many.

The rest of the pack which had been fighting together had killed four, but two of their number had succumbed to the fierce attacks of their opponents, and were dead. Joe and Rob were delighted to know that Bluey and Brutus were all right after the several battles, excepting a few bites which would soon heal.

In taking an inventory of the number of wolves killed by the hounds, they found seven in all. Their hides were so badly torn that they were not worth skinning, so their carcasses were left just where they fell.

It was considered a good morning's work, as it was but eleven o'clock when Cinch had put the finishing touches on his victim. The men were tired after their rough ride, and the hounds slowly followed, tongues out, and many of them limping fearfully. In this way they rode together back to the mouth of the Oxhide, then separated and went to their respective homes.

CHAPTER XIV

WHEN Mr. Tucker, Joe, and Rob arrived at Errolstrath, it was just one o'clock. The family had kept dinner waiting, and everything was ready to put on the table by the time the horses were fed and the hounds' wounds rubbed with witch-hazel. Mrs. Thompson used to prepare this remedy herself, and she considered it the best thing in the world for injuries.

At dinner the boys and the old trapper entertained the family with an account of the morning's hunt, telling them how splendidly both Bluey and Brutus had behaved in company with such thoroughbreds as Custer's hounds, and especially with General Sheridan's famous Cinch, who was supposed to be the finest animal of his kind in the country.

They all adjourned to the broad veranda after

dinner was over, excepting the girls who had to
clear up the things. Mr. Tucker said that
Colonel Keogh had told him that some of the
officers' families who had just come from the East
to Fort Harker were very desirous for wild turkey, which they had not yet tasted.

"He wanted me to ask you, Joe, if you cannot
soon get them a few. I know that this is the
very best time to hunt them, so let you, and
Rob, and me go to that roost on Mud Creek
this evening. It's full moon to-night, and we
shall never have a better chance."

"All right," promptly spoke up both of the
boys. "We'll have to take our ponies," said Joe,
"for it's fully six miles. I was down there the
other afternoon, and I should think that hundreds roost there."

"What time ought we to leave here?" inquired
Rob. "You know that my month to herd and
milk the cows is not out yet, and I want to do
my work before I go; not that father would not
do it willingly for me in a case of this kind, but I
don't care to bother him; he has enough to do
with the other stock."

"Oh!" said Joe, "we need not get away from

here until long after supper. The birds won't come to their roost until it is nearly dark, and as we always have supper at six, and can ride down to Mud Creek easily in an hour, you will have ample time to do your chores, Rob, without hurrying a bit."

" Tell us something about the wild turkey, Mr. Tucker," said Rob. "You know all the habits of our beasts and birds."

" Well, Rob," said the old trapper, "the wild turkey is one of the indigenous birds of America. He once flourished from the most remote eastern boundary of the United States to every part of the far West. Now, through the wantonness of man, he is rapidly disappearing, as is nearly all of our large game. There are still plenty here in Kansas. The wild turkey makes his haunts in the timber, and being gregarious birds they keep together in large flocks, and roost in the same place for years, if not disturbed. All of our domestic turkeys have come from the wild stock, but the wild ones are still larger than the tame ones in many instances. I have shot them in nearly every place in the country where I have hunted. They are stupid in refusing to leave

their roosts at night when shot at. They persistently fly back again to the same trees, when
they could just as easily fly away out of danger.
In such times they are almost as foolish as the
sage hen, which in my opinion is the most stupid
bird that flies. You can shoot at them until you
hit them, if it takes a week; they won't move."

Just as the sun sank behind the hills beyond
the Oxhide bluffs, Joe, Rob, and Mr. Tucker
left Errolstrath for the turkey roost on Mud
Creek. The old trapper rode Joe's buffalo pony,
while Joe mounted the little roan which had
brought his sister so safely from the Indian village; Rob rode Ginger, which Kate had kindly
loaned him for the occasion.

They followed the trail up the creek for about
a mile, then turned abruptly east over the hills
toward Fort Sill military road, then over the
open country for another mile, until they arrived
at the head of Mud Creek.

The moon had risen in a cloudless sky, and
it shines nowhere so brilliantly as in our mid-
continent region. Every tree and bush cast a
shadow, and the trail over the prairie was lighted
up with a golden sheen, so soft and mellow that

Q

you could have seen a pin where the grass had been shorn away.

When they arrived at the edge of the woods in the centre of which was the resting-place of the birds, they tied their ponies to saplings, and then quietly walked on into the timber. As soon as they had come in the vicinity of the roost, they squatted on the ground behind the friendly shelter of a large elm, and waited for the coming of events.

They did not have long to wait. Before they had been there a half an hour, two large flocks came stealthily walking down the deep ravines leading into the sheltered bottom where great trees stood in thick clumps, under whose shadow were the unmistakable signs of an immense roost. At the head of each flock, as it unsuspiciously advanced, strutted a magnificent male bird in all the pride of his leadership. Upon his bronze plumage the moon's rays glinted like a calcium light, as its soft beams sifted through the interstices of the bare limbs of the winter-garbed forest.

When the leader of the flock had arrived at the spot where his charge had been accustomed to roost, he suddenly stopped, glanced cautiously around him for a few seconds, then apparently satisfied that all was right, he gave the signal — a sharp, quick, shrill whistle. At that instant, every bird, with one accord and a tremendous fluttering of wing, raised itself and alighted in the topmost branches of the tallest trees.

In a few moments more, numerous flocks having settled themselves for a peaceful slumber, the old trapper said to the boys: "Now is our time; let's begin!"

Joe had his little Ballard rifle, that had never yet played him false on his hunts with the chief of the Pawnees; Rob had a shot-gun, and Mr. Tucker his never-failing old-fashioned piece which he had carried for twenty-five years.

They fired at first almost simultaneously, but after the first discharge each fired on his own hook. The turkeys fell like the leaves in October. The birds not killed at the first fire did not seem to have sense enough, as Mr. Tucker had said, to escape from their doom. They flew from tree to tree at every shot, persistently remaining in the immediate vicinity of the roost, with all the characteristic idiocy of the sage hen.

When it was time to think of going home, they gathered up their birds, and found they had killed fourteen — more than an average of four apiece. It was all they could do to pack the birds on their ponies, and they were compelled to walk them all the way to the ranche to keep the birds from falling off.

The next morning Joe took the turkeys to Fort Harker, where he disposed of them at a fair price, and received many thanks besides, for his prompt action in response to Colonel Keogh's request to go hunting for them.

CHAPTER XV

THE winter was short, and soon came April,
with its sunny skies. The robins, wrens, blue-
jays, and the mocking-birds made the woods me-
lodious with their sweet notes. The violets by
the brook side under the shade of the great trees
were the first harbingers of the beautiful season,
and the dining-table was made odorous with their
blue blossoms at every meal. Both Kate and
Gertrude loved flowers, and never failed to gather
three times a day, a large bowl full of these
poems of springtime.

Mr. Tucker surprised them one evening by
paying them a visit after a solitary hunting expedition up the creek. The boys soon persuaded
him to stay the night, and tell them a story until
bedtime.

"What shall it be, hunting or fighting?" said Mr. Tucker, turning to Joe.

Before her brother could speak, Gertrude answered for him. "Tell us that legend about the robin, that you have promised us so often."

"Yes, the robin," said Joe. So they all settled into comfortable positions, and Mr. Tucker told them the following story : —

"The Delaware Indians claim that the robin followed them to Kansas. He has been in the eastern part of the state only since the establishment of their reservation within its limits, according to the legend of the tribe.

"The Delawares, you know, were those Indians with whom William Penn made a treaty, the provisions of which were religiously kept for many years.

"Among the Delawares the robin is sacred. From the gray-headed chiefs to the papoose just freed from the thongs of his hard cradle, they all listen with superstitious love and reverence to his warbling. The bird was once the favorite son of a great sachem of that powerful tribe, changed by the Manitou, but still loving man, and evincing it always by building his nest and singing near his abode.

"Once there was, ages ago, a great chief among the Delawares, who then lived in the far East. He was distinguished for his wisdom in the council, and his success in war. He had many wives, but they brought him daughters only, and he, as well as his nation, was dissatisfied, for he desired a son who should succeed to the honorable position of his father.

"One day when the chief was walking through the village, a dove lit on his shoulder, and then flew and nestled in the bosom of a young Indian maiden to whom it belonged. She was the daughter of the medicine-man of the tribe, and her father declared that the dove was a messenger from the Great Spirit, who had thus shown by that sign that the two should be one.

"The news imparted by the medicine-man was agreeable to the chief, for the girl was beautiful and virtuous. He married her, and she became the favorite wife, who, in due time, greatly to his and the joy of his people, presented him with a son. The boy was called Is-a-dill-a, and he grew up different from all the youth of his age; for he was fond of peace, would not mingle with the crowd who tortured prisoners doomed to death, and his father thought him a coward. One day the father upbraided his son for his peaceful inclinations, and Is-a-dill-a answered : —

" 'Great chief of the mighty Delawares, my liver is not white, nor would my blood chill like snow before the enemy, but Is-a-dill-a prefers to gather the wild blossoms which grow upon the prairie, and chase the deer among the cliffs, to lying in ambush for the red man, and sending an arrow into his heart; the Great Spirit, who is father of all the red men, has told me in my dreams to love them all.'

" His father was about to respond angrily to the utterance of a homily so unbecoming a great warrior's son, and the future chief of a powerful tribe, when he saw a huge black bear approaching him with angry demonstrations. The chief was armed, as usual, with bow and arrows, and a stone axe. Is-a-dill-a, without any weapons, was ordered by his father to climb a tree, that he might escape the danger of the impending conflict. The chief, then resting upon one knee, and fixing a selected arrow to his bow, aimed at the eye of the bear, when only a few feet distant. The oscillating motion of the beast's head prevented it from taking fatal effect, and the arrow struck the skull, which was too thick and hard to be penetrated. The now infuriated animal, with a savage growl, sprang upon the chief who dealt it a fearful blow with his stone axe, but was seized in the ponderous paws of the bear, and a mortal struggle ensued. In a moment the chief was bleeding from a hundred wounds, and the animal's mouth was already at his throat, when Is-a-dill-a picked up his father's axe, dealt the beast a powerful blow over the eye, which completely destroyed it, and continued the work until the exhausted animal fell to the earth. But in his death agonies the bear succeeded in embracing Is-a-dill-a and tearing him dreadfully, so that he lay insensible by the side of the dead brute.

"The chief was the first to recover from the swoon in which he had fallen from loss of blood, and as he saw the body of his son lying beside that of the immense bear, it was some time before he could connect the circumstances, for it appeared impossible for a boy of his age to perform such an exploit. He was bitterly grieved, when he thought how pure was the filial affection of his son, and bitterly regretted the reproaches he had often heaped upon him who was so worthy of honor and affection. He crawled to his son's body, — for he believed him dead, — but feeling that the heart was still beating, with much effort and great pain he succeeded in getting some water from a little spring near by, and applied it to the forehead and lips of the insensible Is-a-dill-a; in a few moments he gave a deep sigh, looked at his father with a glow of recognition, then again became unconscious.

"Fortunately at this moment, three squaws who had been gathering berries, approached, and seeing the condition of the chief and his son, hastened to the village for assistance. By careful nursing, both recovered, and the boy became the object of admiration and reverence; for since his exploit with the bear, none dare dispute his courage, which is the greatest virtue among the Indians.

"As I have already told you, it is necessary for all promising youths to retire into some solitary place, and submit to a long fast, that they may propitiate the Great Spirit. In a few years, Is-a-dill-a expressed his desire to attempt the ordeal. The chief made everything in

readiness, and soon Is-a-dill-a was alone in his
little lodge in the wilderness, upon his bed of
skin. He looked up with great confidence to the
Great Spirit, and felt that the light of his countenance would rest upon him. Every morning
his father visited him, and encouraged him to
persevere, by appealing to his pride, his ambition,
and his noble instincts. The ninth day came
and passed, and also the tenth; on the morning
of the eleventh Is-a-dill-a was dying with weak-
ness, and his full, rounded muscles had shrunk
and withered from the prostrating effects of the
terrible ordeal.

"'Father,' said the almost expiring youth, 'I
have fasted eleven days, a longer time than man
ever fasted before; the Great Spirit is satisfied;
give me something to eat that I may not die.'

"'To-morrow, my son, before the bright sun
rises, I will bring you venison cooked by your
mother; fast until then that your name may
become mighty among the great chiefs of the
Delawares.'

"The old man departed, proud of the fame his
son would acquire; and the next morning, before
the sun had risen, he was at the lodge of Is-a-

dill-a, with a supply of the most tempting food; but he stood motionless before a strange sight within the lodge. There was a youth with golden wings and most beautiful features, having a halo of light around his head, painting the breast of Is-a-dill-a with vermilion, and his body brown. Then, in a moment, the winged youth was changed to a dove, and Is-a-dill-a to a strange and beautiful bird, and they both flew through the door of the lodge to a tree, and the strange bird thus addressed the chief of the Delawares:

" 'Father, farewell. The Great Spirit, when he saw that I was dying from hunger, sent a messenger for me, and I am changed to this bird. I will always preserve my love for man, and will build and carol near his dwelling.'

" The two birds then flew away, but every morning the robin, during the lifetime of the chief, sang from the large oak tree that overshadowed his lodge.

" When the Delawares moved west of the Missouri, the faithful descendants of the strange bird followed them, and that is how the robins came to Kansas."

The mocking-bird, that sweetest of our feath-

ered songsters, is indigenous to the central
region of the great plains, and his notes are
heard when the day breaks. He seeks the highest points upon the dwellings, the ridge of the
house, the barn, or the top of the windmill, if
there be one, where, like the Aztecs of old, or
their lineal descendants, the Pueblo Indians of
New Mexico to-day, he greets the coming god
in the east.

Like the robin, the mocking-bird loves the
companionship of man. He builds his nest near
their dwellings, in the garden, the orchard, or
the trees close by. Kate and Gertrude had
made several attempts to get hold of some little
ones in their nests, but there was always something that seemed to thwart their plans. Last
year they found a nest in a grapevine in the
garden, and they watched it zealously day by
day, from the laying of the last twig by the
parent birds, to the hatching of the two white
eggs. They saw the fledglings develop from
week to week, until they were nearly large
enough to be taken from the nest, when one
morning, on going as usual to watch the prog-
ress of the little birds, what was their horror to

see a snake swallowing the last one. The other, they knew, by the swelled body of the reptile, was hopelessly gone! Their disgust and sorrow may be imagined, and as it was too late in the season to think of finding another nest with young ones in it, they were forced to abandon their quest until another spring.

This April they were successful. A pair had built their nest in the vine-covered summer-house, a rustic little place that Mr. Thompson had erected out of the wild grape, for a retreat in which his wife and daughters might sit in the afternoons when they did not care to go as far as the deep woods. No harm came to the fledglings this time, and they were placed in a handsome cage bought by the girls from the proceeds of the eggs laid by their own brown Leghorn hens.

The birds soon became very tame, and made the house resonant all day long with their brilliant notes. They knew the girls the moment they came near the cage, and would stretch their wings and gently pick at their fingers when they put them between the wires. They were a constant source of pleasure, for the girls loved pets of all kinds, and taught them to return their affection by means of gentleness and constant kindness.

Joe lost his elk this spring, and he was greatly disturbed by it. He had made arrangements with an old hunter, living near Fort Harker, to go out to the Saline Valley and capture another young one. He intended to break them both to harness, and expected to have a unique team to drive. The elk was so tame that he permitted it to roam at will through the woods on the margin of the Oxhide, where it browsed on the small bushes or grazed on the luxurious grass which grew in such profusion on the creek bottom. It always returned to the corral at night for its feed of corn, but one evening it failed to come up as usual. He wandered through the woods, looking for it, when, happening to come upon a camp near the mouth of the Oxhide on the trail westward, he saw to his indignation, that the emigrants, a very ignorant set from Missouri, had butchered his elk. He gave them a talking-to that was more emphatic than choice in its language. They told him they thought it was a wild one, but he became disgusted at their

falsehood, and asked them if wild elks had blue
ribbons on their necks as his had, and he pulled
it from the hide which was lying near their wagons. The girls had sewed it on the elk for him
not a week ago. He saw that the party was
such a miserable set that he could do nothing
with them, so he had to leave the place, as mad
as a wet hen, and abandon his idea of ever having an elk team.

It was a relief for the family to feel that they
could now go where they pleased without fear of
marauding bands of Indians. The winter campaign had most effectually settled their propensi-
ties for murdering and scalping the settlers, so
both the girls and boys made trips to the neighbors, and went on fishing excursions, or hunted
whenever they cared to. Even the wolves,
which had been such a terror to the whole
neighborhood, had been so successfully thinned
out in several " surrounds " by the men living on
the various creeks, that the raspberry patch was
no longer infested by them.

Kate and her sister went up there one morning, not expecting, of course, that the berries
would be ripe as early as April. As neither of

them had visited the place since Kate's capture, and everything was now perfectly safe, they thought they would like to go there again.

When they arrived at the well-remembered ledge of rocks, Kate pointed out to Gertrude the exact spot where she was standing when the savages swooped down on her; and they climbed to the top where they were attacked by the wolf.

They found the vines full of blossoms, promising a beautiful crop in June, and while strolling along the bank of the stream they suddenly came upon a quail's nest in which twenty-five eggs were just hatching out. As the quail runs the moment it breaks from the shell, the girls determined to take the little ones home and bring them up as they did their chickens. The old birds made a terrible fuss. They would run a short distance from the nest, and pretend to be very lame; apparently being hardly able to move. They thus tried to induce the girls to catch them—a ruse adopted by many other birds when their young ones are in danger. But Kate and Gertrude, who were well posted in the tricks of animals and birds, paid no attention to the

R

antics of the old quails, but were intent on catching all of the little ones they could. Even then
it was a hard job, for the baby quails run almost
as fast as the parents, and hide in the grass
where they lie quiet until all danger is past.
They succeeded, however, in getting all but four
of them, and walked hurriedly back to Errolstrath
with the tender things in their aprons.

" If I didn't know they were quails," said Kate,
" I should think that they were young brown
Leghorn chickens. Did you ever see such a
resemblance, Gert ? "

" They do look exactly like the brown Leghorns, and do you know, Kate, that when I first
saw a brood of Leghorns, I thought they were
young quails."

" I expect we shall have little trouble in rais-
ing them, for Jenny Campbell had as many as
a dozen of them in her cellar all last summer.
Her brother caught them as we did these, in
the spring, just as they were coming out of
their shells. They will eat small grain like
chickens."

" Well, we won't keep them in our cellar,"
said Gertrude; " we'll get Joe or Rob to build

us a big cage out of lath, and then we can
make them as tame as the mocking-birds."

"Do you purpose to eat them?" inquired Kate.

"Certainly; why not? Mamma and papa love
them broiled on toast, and so do I. I don't
expect to make such pets of them that when
the time comes to eat them, I shall think so
much of them that I can't do it; and you must
not either, Kate."

The girls arrived safely at the ranche with
their charge, and Joe being begged to make a
cage, set about it at once, and had it ready in
less than an hour. The birds were put in it,
and it was set on the veranda, where the little
things could get plenty of air and sunlight.
They picked up millet seed as readily as an
old chicken, when Gertrude threw in a handful
to them. In a few days they were contented
in their confinement and became very tame.

Kate and her sister intended to raise a great
many chickens this spring, and they set as
many as forty hens; for their eggs and young
broilers brought a good price at the fort and
in the village. They had excellent luck at
hatching time, but as the little ones began to

grow, when the girls counted them every morning they found their number decreasing day by day. They could not divine the cause at first, so Rob was set to watch, and discover, if he could, what caused their disappearance. Some hens that had fifteen or sixteen would come around the yard next morning with only six or seven.

They had three cats: one named Dame Trot, a pure tabby; one called Mischief, a white and gray; and Tortoise, because of her color. Tortoise had a litter of kittens which she kept under the front porch. Joe had suspected that the cats knew something of the disappearance of the little birds, and told Rob to keep his eyes on them. As he sat one evening on the veranda he saw Tortoise suddenly spring from behind a cherry tree and catch one of the young Leghorns in her mouth and carry it to her nest under the porch. Rob immediately crawled there, and to his surprise found the heads of more than twenty chickens. He ran into the house and told of his discovery. His father said that the cat must be killed at once; for when a cat gets a taste for chickens, it is impossible to break it of the habit, and Joe

was commissioned to put the guilty Tortoise
out of the way.

Kate cried and was in great distress, for Tortoise was her cat, and she begged her father to
put off its death until to-morrow morning, when
she would go and spend the day with Jenny
Campbell. She could not bear to stay and see
her favorite cat killed. Her request was granted,
and Tortoise had a respite until morning, but
she was shut up in a box so that she could not
get any more of the chickens.

When morning came, Kate got Rob to saddle
Ginger, but before she started she begged Joe
to bury Tortoise in some out of the way place
where she would never find her grave. Joe
promised he would, and when his sister was out
of sight down the trail, he took the cat out of
her prison and went to the woodpile, and with
one stroke of the axe cut off her head. Then
he took her down into the woods and buried
her under a bunch of wild plum bushes, where
no one would ever see the grave.

After the death of Tortoise the chickens
throve admirably, and no more were ever missed
by reason of the cats having caught them.

CHAPTER XVI

THE PAWNEES RETURN — ANTELOPE HUNT WITH THE INDIANS —
JOE MISSES — WHITE WOLF — TALK OF A WILD HORSE HUNT
— THE SAND-HILL CRANES — THEIR WEIRD COTILLION

THE Pawnees camped on the Oxhide that autumn earlier than usual, as one of the boys of the tribe had said they would.

The band arrived the first week in September, and Joe was again in his element. He spent every spare moment in the camp, but, much to his regret, learned that his old friend Yellow-Calf was dead; he had died about a month before of sheer wearing out. He was nearer ninety than eighty, which he had given as his age to Joe. One of the younger of the principal men had been made chief in his place. He had been with the band every season when they camped on the creek, and also was a firm friend to Joe, so the boy had lost nothing except the presence of the old fellow who thought so much of him.

One morning about the middle of April while the Indians were still on the Oxhide, and Joe as usual was in the camp, a warrior came in and reported a large herd of antelope on the Smoky Hill bottom; he said there were at least eight hundred of them. He proposed to Joe that they should go after them, and the boy agreed without any hesitation.

The chief told them they had better take about half a dozen of the men with them; for if the antelope were out on the open prairie, they could not get near enough to them without a great deal of trouble. If they had some one to drive the herd toward them while they hid themselves in the tall grass, they could entice a number within range by using the usual strategy.

Joe and the Indian, whose name was the White Wolf, started, taking with them seven men of the band as drivers. When they got out into the opening beyond the timber on the Oxhide, they discovered the large herd unsuspiciously grazing about two miles away.

The seven Indians were then ordered to make a détour far beyond the animals, at least a mile from the far side of them, while Joe and White

Wolf secreted themselves in a large patch of bunch-grass. This was out on the prairie about a hundred rods distant from the timber, and was pointed to by White Wolf so that his men would understand exactly what was required of them.

Joe and the Indian who had remained behind with him, then walked leisurely toward the bunch of tall grass. They had plenty of time to prepare themselves, as it would take at least an hour before the Indians could get beyond the herd to move it.

On the way to the prairie Joe had stopped at the ranch, to borrow the Spencer carbine for White Wolf, while he took his little Ballard rifle, that was only good for about a hundred and fifty yards, while the Spencer would carry a ball five hundred.

They reached their hiding-place in plenty of time, for they lay there fully fifteen minutes before they saw a commotion among the antelope. The herd were observed to raise their heads as if they winded danger, and then making a few of their characteristic stiff-legged bounds, they stood alert as if preparing for flight.

Joe knew by this that the animals had been

startled by the Indians, though he could not see
a sign of one of them.

The herd at first ran as swiftly as they could
in an easterly direction, then they began to
slacken their pace, and a few, having recovered
their courage, commenced to nibble gingerly at
the short buffalo grass again. At this juncture
White Wolf tied a white rag around his head,
and, standing on his knees, began to sway his
body backward and forward with a steady oscillating motion. Presently the antelope saw him,
and a few of them stopped short to gaze at the
strange object.

In a few moments four or five of the inquisitive creatures moved slowly forward again, still
attracted by the swaying white figure of the savage, which so excited their curiosity. Presently,
as they came closer and closer, Joe told White
Wolf not to fire until they came within range of
his little gun. Soon the proper distance was
attained, and Joe, drawing up his piece, said: —

"Now, White Wolf, fire away!"

Their pieces were discharged simultaneously;
it seemed like a single shot, so accurately had
the triggers been pulled together. Two of the

graceful creatures rolled over on their sides, one, White Wolf's, instantly killed, while Joe's was sprawling out, every limb quivering like an aspen leaf.

Both hunters dropped their guns and started out to cut the throats of their game. Joe was in the act of placing his hand on the neck of the one he had fired at, when, to his surprise, it jumped to its feet and ran off to join its not far-away companions, and the astonished boy never saw it again!

Which was the more surprised, the boy or the antelope, it would be difficult to determine. He turned to the savage, who was bewildered, too, and asked him what in the world was the cause of the animal's recovery after he had shot him.

"I aimed at his heart as he stood broadside toward me," said Joe, "and I don't know what it means."

"You only grazed him," answered White Wolf. "We Indians often catch wild horses in that way, when we can't get them in any other." Of course, they conversed in the Pawnee tongue, for the savage did not understand a word of English.

"Oh! I know what you mean, White Wolf," said Joe. "I just grazed his spinal cord with the ball; it paralyzed him for a moment, that's all. Yellow Calf told me how the Pawnees used to catch wild horses in that way, down on the Cimarron bottom, when the tribe lived on the Republican River."

"I'm soon going down there with some of my warriors. A Kaw brave told me the other day that there are a good many wild horses there yet; will you go, too?" asked White Wolf of his young friend.

"I'll go if my father and mother are willing, and I guess they will be," replied Joe. "I should so like to see a herd of wild horses. I have seen nearly all the other animals that live on the plains and in the timber, but have never seen wild horses, because they don't range as far east as Oxhide Creek. There are lots of them in Nebraska though, farther north, Mr. Tucker says."

As the prairie was too level for the hunters to hope to get near the antelope again, now that they had discharged their pieces, and as the other Indians were coming up to them, they decided to go back.

One of White Wolf's men packed the dead
antelope on his horse, and they all rode slowly
toward Errolstrath. When they arrived there,
White Wolf insisted that Joe take half of the
game. To this at first the boy did not agree,
but as the chief insisted so persistently, he finally
consented. So the antelope was divided fairly,
one portion was carried into the house, and the
other to the Indian camp down the creek.

At dinner Joe told his father that White Wolf
was going to the Cimarron bottom in a few days
to try to capture some wild horses which, so he
learned from one of his Kaw friends, were roam-
ing on the salt marshes of that region, and that
the chief wanted him to go with him.

Mr. Thompson said that he had not the slightest objection now that the war was over and there
was nothing to be feared from the savages, but
he told Joe that if any animals were captured, he
ought to be entitled to a share.

"I have made that all right with White Wolf
already, father," said Joe. "He agrees to give me
as great a proportion as his other warriors are
entitled to. He hopes to capture at least one
apiece, as the Kaw who told him about the herd

said there were three or four hundred of them down there."

As soon as dinner was over, Joe jumped on his pony and loped off to the Indian camp to tell White Wolf that he could go to hunt wild horses with the band.

The chief said that he was glad of it, and that they would start by the first of the week. It was now Thursday, and that would give them all plenty of time to make ready. He told Joe that he would let him have a pony out of his herd, so that he could save his own the hard trip, for there would be severe work for all the ponies.

Joe started back to the ranche, and when he arrived at the foot of Haystack Mound, on the side of it farthest from the corral, he saw a squadron of sand-hill cranes circling around near the ground, and as he knew they were going to alight, he pulled up his pony. After turning loose his animal, which he knew would run right to the corral, he hid himself in the plum bushes which grew all over the bottom, to watch the strange antics of those curious birds.

They dance a regular cotillion when on the

ground. They chassez backward and forward, and waltz around, keeping time in a rude sort of way as they go through the mazes of their weird movements.

Presently they all came fluttering down, about forty of them, and immediately began their laughable capers. Joe had witnessed their performance a hundred times, but he could never resist looking at it again whenever the opportunity offered. They danced for more than half an hour, and then seeming to have enjoyed themselves sufficiently, they took flight, and soon were but as a wreath of dark blue far up in the sky.

Joe returned to the house, and puttered around until supper was ready. At the table he told of his stopping at Haystack Mound to witness the antics of a flock of cranes that had alighted on the sand knoll near there, and said he could sit and look at them all day.

Of course all the family had witnessed the performance of the cranes often, for in the season scarcely a day passed that a flock did not make its appearance somewhere on the ranche.

Kate said, " I used to watch them on the Canadian when I was in the Indian village, and

they were about the only things that I laughed
at while there.   After I had been there about
a month and had got pretty well acquainted, one
of the boys gave me a young crane for a pet.
He became so tame that he would follow me all
over the village.

"I kept him three months, when one morning,
as I was walking down to the river with him,
I saw him suddenly stop, put his head on one
side, look up at the sky, and running a few
steps, fly away.   I watched him until he was
out of sight.   It was a flock of his own species
that he had seen, and I did not even begin to
hear their croaking until he was far out of
sight."

CHAPTER XVII

THE Pawnees remained on Oxhide Creek later than usual this spring. As they wanted to go on a hunt for the wild horses on the Cimarron bottom, they had to wait until the grass grew enough to furnish pasture for their own ponies on the trip.

About the middle of April, White Wolf told his warriors that he would start in a few days. A runner was despatched to Errolstrath, to tell Joe the band would leave in a short time, and to be ready at a moment's notice. The runner said that when White Wolf started he wanted to be off very early in the morning, so as to make the Arkansas the first night.

Joe, all anxious for the exciting trip, persuaded his mother and sisters to bake up a lot of bread,

and boil hard a couple of dozen eggs for him.
He told them that that would be all he wanted,
as they intended to depend upon the chase,
Indian fashion, for everything else; and as the
country they were going over was full of buffalo,
antelope, and elk, they would not suffer from
lack of food.

He cleaned his father's Spencer carbine, bought
a box of cartridges for it, and told Kate that
he intended to ride the roan which she got
from the Indians and had given to him. He
thought the animal was better than any the
Pawnees had in their herd, though White Wolf
had said that he could ride one of theirs.

The night of the third day after the runner
had come to tell Joe to get ready, another one
came to the ranche and said that White Wolf
and the warriors would start in the morning.
He told him that he had better come to the
camp with him, and stay there that night, so that
there would be no delay about getting off early
in the morning. So Joe got his things ready,
tied a couple of blankets to the cantle of his
saddle, his lariat to the horn; slung his carbine
over his shoulder, and buckled his belt of car-

s

tridges around his waist. He then bade good by
to the family, jumped on his pony, which he
had named Comanche, after the tribe which had
captured Kate, and rode with the runner who had
come for him, to the Pawnee camp a mile distant.

Arriving there, Joe found everything in con-
fusion. Some of the warriors were picketing
their riding animals near the tepees, allowing
the loose ponies to run at large, as they will
never leave the main bunch. Others were packing their wallets of par-flèche with dried meat
for the journey. White Wolf was sitting in the
door of his lodge, smoking his pipe and giving
general directions to his warriors.

At last everything was straightened out to
the satisfaction of the chief, and then all adjourned to their several tepees to make ready
their arms and ropes for the work that was to
be done when they reached the Cimarron.

Joe slept in the lodge of the chief that night,
and before the dawn was fairly upon the world,
the warriors were up, saddling their ponies, taking down their lodges, and packing their traps
on the backs of the animals designated for that
purpose. Then after a hastily swallowed break-

fast of dried buffalo meat, at a signal from White Wolf, the party mounted, and the cavalcade rode southwest at a gentle lope, the pack animals in front, in charge of two warriors.

Joe rode alongside of White Wolf in the centre of the column, and they talked of the probability of finding the herd of wild horses on the salt marsh where they were going.

They pulled up about noon to graze their animals and to have a smoke, which is the first thing an Indian does when he halts: it is of more importance to him than eating.

The Big Bend where the Pawnees wished to cross the Arkansas was seventy-two miles from the Oxhide, near the famous Pawnee Rock, on the old Santa Fé Trail.

When the sun was about two hours high, they could see, three or four miles distant, the white contour of the sand hills which border the great silent, treeless stream, and the Indians knew that their camping-ground was near. It was to be in the timber at the mouth of the Walnut, less than two miles from the spot where they would strike the Arkansas.

Before it had grown fairly dark, the heavy

timber on the Walnut was reached, and the party halted, turned their animals loose, took another smoke, and then prepared for the night.

Around the camp-fire, White Wolf and several of the oldest warriors told how that region once belonged to their tribe. Their largest village had been two hundred miles farther north, on the Republican, and many times they had come down to where they were now camped, to hunt the buffalo, or steal horses from the Cheyennes, their hereditary enemies. They told how they were once a powerful nation, but the white man had stolen their lands, and now, only a small band, they were obliged to live on a reservation set apart for them by the Government.

It was a wild region where Joe now found himself. All night long could be heard the cry of the lynx, which sounded like that of an infant. The wolves howled in the timbered recesses of the creek, but Joe slept well, rolled up in his blankets in the chief's lodge, and it was morning before he thought he had been asleep an hour.

At the first streak of dawn, the Indians were

out. White Wolf said that the mouth of the
Walnut used to be a favorite place for elk. They
might still haunt the stream; he would send out
some of his hunters, and perhaps they would
have elk for their breakfast.

He selected two of the warriors, who started
out on foot to see if they could find any game.
Joe, of course, accompanied them. They stalked
cautiously as only an Indian can — Joe had
mastered the art perfectly — along the bank of
the stream, not a stick breaking under their feet,
nor the sound of the rustle of a dead leaf being
heard, so quietly did they tread.

At last, arriving at a bend of the creek, where
the timber grows the thickest, the Indian in the
lead stopped abruptly, put his hand out behind
him, the sign for the others to halt, and taking
Joe's carbine from the boy's shoulder, got down
on his belly and crawled forward as noiselessly
as a snake. Suddenly he raised the gun, and
seeming to take a careless aim, pulled the trigger,
and immediately Joe and the other warrior saw
four elk rush past them, down the prairie, and
out of sight.

As he turned to Joe and the other warrior,

telling them at the same time to come on, the Indian who had fired said in his own language, " We'll have elk for breakfast now."

They followed him into the timber, and there, not thirty yards from where he had stood when he fired the carbine, was an elk, about two years old, dead as a stone wall !

The work of skinning the elk did not take more than ten minutes, and it was cut up into conveniently sized pieces, and each one of the hunters packed his portion to camp, less than a mile distant.

When they arrived they found the fire burning briskly, for White Wolf and the other warriors had heard the report of the gun, and they knew that something in the shape of game had been secured, for Mazakin and Trotter, the two Indians whom the chief had sent out, were unfailing shots. The meat was soon cut into slices, and each man cut a twig fork upon which he stuck a slice, and every one became a cook for himself. Joe produced a loaf of his bread, and with water alone for drink they made an excellent meal.

When they had finished, the sun was just rising like a great molten ball out of the horizon of the far-stretching level prairie. The ponies, standing ready, were mounted, and the party moved out, crossed the Arkansas at Pawnee Rock, and continued a southwesterly course all day.

By sundown they arrived at the Cimarron, a clear, babbling stream, where the water was a little brackish, and which the Cheyennes call Ho-to-oa-oa (Buffalo).

There were no trees at this part of the Cimarron in those days, and they were obliged to pitch their camp on the sandy bank of the river. The grass was luxurious, and their animals fairly revelled in it. They soon filled themselves and lay down, as if they realized the hard work which would be their portion for the next few days.

There were plenty of fish in the river, and as Joe had thoughtfully brought some hooks and lines, he and White Wolf with two of the other warriors took dried buffalo meat for bait, and soon caught all they wanted for their supper.

The next morning they broke camp at daybreak, and rode for a grove of timber just visible in the far-distant western horizon, where White Wolf said he believed they would find some wild horses. They always take shelter at night in timber if any is to be found, and wander out on the prairie in the morning to graze.

The party arrived at the grove by two o'clock, and established their permanent camp, as they saw the unmistakable signs that a herd of wild horses made it their nightly rendezvous. Their lodges were put up in the southern edge of the grove, away from the trails of the animals.

The Indians kept very quiet all day, sitting in the shadow of their lodges, smoking and talking. They did not even build any fires, but contented themselves with their dried buffalo meat and the bread which Joe had brought, for fear of making the slightest disturbance, and thus preventing the wild horses from returning to their usual nightly resting-place. Every once in a while, either White Wolf himself or some of the other warriors would venture out of the timber and gaze long and anxiously over the vast prairie, in hope of seeing something of the bunch, which they knew was grazing somewhere not many miles away. Once the chief thought he saw in the distance, moving objects which he took for horses, for he was noted far beyond any other

member of his band for his keen sight. He was
right in his conjectures, for before half an hour had
passed from the time he had first riveted his attention, the bunch — for such it was — had swung
around, broadside to, and, approaching nearer
the timber, could be counted. There were over
forty animals, led by a magnificent black horse
which the chief said he would try to capture.

It was a beautiful sight, and Joe stood trans-
fixed as they kicked up their heels, and raced
after one another like a group of school children,
little suspecting that, before the sun went down
the next evening, many of them would be ridden
by the Indians who were now gazing at them so
covetously.

Night seemed to be very slow in coming to
the band of Pawnees, who smoked and smoked
incessantly, to pass the long hours before darkness would invite the herd to seek its bed-ground.
At last after dark, by the light of the crescent
moon, they saw the animals, led by the coal-black
stallion, cautiously walk into the timber about a
mile from the Pawnee camp. When the neighing
and pawing had ceased, the hunters wrapped
themselves in their blankets and buffalo robes,

intending to be up before it was light, and surprise the herd before it was ready to go out to
graze.

The ponies were securely picketed, saddles,
girths, and bridles examined, buffalo-hair lariats
overhauled, and all made ready for an early start
on the hard day's ride.

Long before the sun had showed the faintest
indication of his coming; while the stars were
still shining brilliantly, the Indians and Joe were
up, and hastily breakfasting, or taking their matu-
tinal smoke. They then mounted their ponies,
and stealthily walked the animals in the direction
of the slumbering bunch of wild horses.

When they had arrived within a few hundred
yards of the place where the handsome creatures
were still unconsciously resting, one of the Indians and Joe, who was as good as the best man
among them, dismounted and crawled forward in
the brush to reconnoitre. They returned in a
few moments and reported to White Wolf that
all was quiet, not a single horse's ear had they
seen pricked up, so the animals had not as yet
been warned of danger.

White Wolf then gave his orders, making such

disposition of his forces as would cause the herd to be surrounded when the warriors had approached near enough to use their lassoes. So quietly did the ponies do their duty, that when the herd was awakened to hear and see their enemies almost upon them, the lassoes of several of the warriors had done their work.

As the others bounded away with astonishing speed, out of the timber and over the prairie, a spirited chase commenced. The Pawnees urged their ponies to their greatest capacity, the manes and tails of the wild horses in front were flying wildly in the air, while their hoofs were beating the hard sod, showing how tightly strung were the muscles of the frightened animals.

The Pawnees were obviously gaining upon the fugitives, quick-footed though they were. The chief came up with the leader, the splendid black stallion, and began to swing his lasso around his head, gradually enlarging the circles by permitting the rough buffalo-rope to slip gently through his fingers. A sudden movement at the same instant plunged the stallion into an increased speed, when, White Wolf thumping the flanks of his mettlesome pony, it dashed quickly forward, and the Pawnee threw his lariat with unerring skill around the neck of the black horse. The bunch was thrown into a panic, when the members of it saw their leader tumble to the ground, and wheeling round in their course, they were completely surrounded by their pursuers. At least ten were lassoed by the same number of Pawnees, including Joe, who had long ago become an expert with the rope. The remainder of the bunch not yet caught were kept together by the rest of the Indians, who were continually circling around them, so that not one escaped, and at the end of an hour the whole forty were lassoed, and tied fast by the legs. Some fifteen of them were not desirable animals, and these were turned loose again.

The business of breaking them in began when they had driven the remaining twenty-five to their camp down on the farther edge of the grove. The frightened animals, notwithstanding their fetters of rawhide, kicked up the earth, shook their heavy manes, curved their necks, and, with eyes that seemed all afire, gazed tremblingly at their captors.

As White Wolf wanted the black stallion for

his own riding, he began with him. It took four of the stoutest Pawnees to hold the fiery creature by a long lasso; this had the effect of partial strangulation, which weakened and temporarily overcame the wonderful power of the spirited creature. Violent were his plunges as he tried to free himself from the grasp of his captors. His terrific leaps only served to draw the lariat tighter around his neck; his breathing became more and more difficult, and might have been heard for the eighth of a mile. His heart beat as if it would burst from his heaving chest, and his veins stood out in great ridges along his quivering flesh.

At last, overwhelmed by his agony and fear, powerless with suffocation, he fell, and for an instant lay upon the ground without sense or motion. The lariat was immediately loosened around his neck, and as consciousness returned to him, his already glazed eyes became bright again, the fresh air dilated his nostrils, and his tremendous chest rose and fell.

In ten minutes he was on his feet, but how different he appeared from the magnificent animal which had stood in all his native pride and

dignity at the head of his band. He was weak,
hardly able to stand, his great head drooped, and
his eyes were without that natural brilliancy
which had so markedly characterized them; he
appeared only the ghost of his former self. Like
a monarch who had been dragged from his throne,
who has been scoffed at by those whom he had
previously despised, he was destined to become
the slave of man.

As soon as the horse somewhat recovered
from his exhaustion, he was mounted by White
Wolf, who kept his seat, notwithstanding the
animal's terrific efforts to throw him, and forced
him to run round and round in a circle. If for a
moment the horse showed the slightest mani-
festation of flagging or obstinacy, White Wolf
would give him an awful blow over the head with
his heavy buffalo-hair rope. Gradually he became more passive, and in less than half an hour
from the time when the chief had mounted him,
he was declared broken, and was led away to be
picketed with the rest of the Indian ponies.

The remaining twenty-four horses were all subjected to the same course of discipline; some
giving up in a few moments, others as obstinate

as was their leader. Before dark all had been sufficiently subdued to suit a savage's idea of gentleness, and the party went to bed that night elated over their wonderful success.

The next morning they started for home, camping at the same place on the Walnut. From there to the Oxhide, they made two night halts instead of one, as on their outward trip.

Joe's share of the capture was three beautiful ponies. Under the discipline of the kindness which always prevailed at Errolstrath, these were made in a few weeks almost as gentle as tame horses.

CHAPTER XVIII

THE LAST HERD OF BUFFALO — THE STAMPEDE — THE SOLDIERS
IN FULL CHASE — JOE GETS TWO COWS — HAULING IN THE
MEAT — RATTLESNAKES

THE last big herd of buffalo ever seen in the
valley of the Oxhide visited their ancient feeding-
grounds during that same spring of 1869, when
Joe hunted wild horses on the Cimarron with the
Pawnees. One morning, shortly after his return
to Errolstrath, an immense number of the shaggy
ruminants came tearing across the Smoky Hill,
below the fort. They rushed up toward the
soldiers' barracks, and dashed wildly through
the post, over the parade-ground, and on toward
the Oxhide.

In a moment the whole garrison was in full
chase, enlisted men and officers, and a fusillade
ensued, which sounded at a distance like a general engagement of troops. The firing was heard
on the Oxhide, and several of the Pawnees who
happened to be out on the highest bluffs saw the

"The last big herd of buffalo ever seen in the valley of the Oxhide."

herd coming. One of their number hurried to
their camp and notified the other warriors, who
immediately mounted their ponies and got ready
for the chase. Joe and Rob were hunting rabbits
with their hounds that morning on an elevated
plateau, and they, too, saw the cloud of dust raised
by the great herd, as it came thundering through
the Smoky Hill bottom. Forgetting all about
rabbits and everything else, they rushed to the
house for their guns. In a few moments they
joined the Indians, who were coming at a breakneck gait toward the on-rushing mass. The
buffalo, wild with fear and excitement at their
proximity to the cabins of the settlers, were on a
general stampede.

When buffalo are stampeded, they become
absolutely blind, and rush without any aim into
anything that is in their path. Some of the
frightened beasts that now had reached Errolstrath ranche, dashed through the front yard,
leaping over fences and gates as easily as a
greyhound. In their mad career they knocked
down the milk-pans, water-buckets, and other
things that stood near the kitchen door.

Kate was standing on the wash-bench, trying

T

to get a good look at the buffalo as they came
tearing along, and before she was aware of the
fact, she found herself sprawling on the ground.
An old bull that was separated from the rest of
the herd had come dashing round the corner of
the house, and striking the end of the bench with
his leg, sent Kate headlong. She picked herself
up unhurt, and rushed into the house, almost as
badly scared as when the Cheyennes had swooped
down on her.

She gathered her wits in a moment, and with
her mother and sister stood on the back veranda, where they could all see the herd now far
up on the hills, and still running in their madness. The Indians, soldiers, and officers were
shooting at the frenzied beasts as they ran
among them, regardless of consequences. Now
and then they toppled one of the huge animals
over, but the white men in their excitement
missed oftener than they hit, while the Pawnees
rarely failed to bring down their game.

The party on the porch at Errolstrath watched
the herd and hunters until nothing but a cloud
of dust could be seen far in the distance, yet
the yelling of the Pawnees could still be faintly

heard long after the buffalo had vanished from sight.

By noon, Indians and whites slowly retraced their course down to the creek bottom, the Pawnees going to their camp, the soldiers to the fort, and the boys, Joe and Rob, home.

" How many of the buffalo were killed after all that terrible yelling and shooting ? " asked their mother.

" Well, not nearly as many as ought to have been," answered Joe. " I never saw such a mixed-up mess in all my life. Enough cartridges were used to have killed five hundred, but the men from the fort were as excited as the buffalo, and they didn't hit an animal once in a hundred shots, and then when they did, half the time the ball struck them where it had no more effect than if you had hit them with a stick !

" The Pawnees killed more than all the others; they got twenty-five, and have gone to camp for ponies to pack the meat on. I don't think that fifty buffaloes were killed in all. I got two, both of 'em cows, and I must take the wagon out and haul 'em in. We will have enough meat to last us a long while, but we shall have to smoke most of it."

"Where did the herd go?" inquired Kate.

"Most of the animals kept right on toward the east, while some of them turned round and travelled south. I suspect that the settlers on Plum Creek flats will have a good time with them, as a part of the herd that went south was headed for there. I tell you," continued Joe, "you've got to keep a clear head on your shoulders when you go after buffalo. Most of those fellows from Fort Harker are recruits, and are fresh from the East; they never saw a buffalo before, and I don't wonder they were excited."

"I never saw so many rattlesnakes," said Rob, "as I did on that big stony prairie where we killed the majority of the buffalo. I guess I counted fifty if I did one. I think that the stamping of the buffalo must have frightened them out of their holes."

"It's very lucky that the rattlesnakes out here are not so venomous as those back East," said Mrs. Thompson; "more than twenty persons have been bitten by them in the neighborhood since we've lived here, and a little whiskey soon cures it."

"Do you remember, Gert," said Kate, "when you nearly sat down on one that was curled up on that stump you were going to take for a seat in the woods last autumn, and he rattled just in time ? "

" I guess I do," answered her sister. " There's one thing I like about a rattlesnake : he always gives you good warning that he is around. He doesn't ever take you unawares, like some animals, a bull dog for instance, that says nothing, and takes hold of you before you know it."

" Their skins make pretty belts and hatbands," said Rob. " The cowboys on the big cattle ranches kill hundreds of them while they are out herding, and tan the skins to put around their hats. I saw a whole set of jewelry that was made out of the rattles and mounted with gold wire. One of the boys was going to send it to Texas to his sister."

" Well, they may be odd," said Mrs. Thompson, " but I certainly shouldn't like to wear them."

" I like the furs of animals better than anything for ornament, either to wear or to have in my room," said Kate. " I guess it would make a city girl envious to see my chamber with all its beautiful skins that Joe and Rob have given me. One of these days I mean to have

papa send some of those otter and beaver skins
to Kansas City, and get them made up into a cape
and muff."

"He will," said her mother. "I was telling
your father only the other day when we were up
in your room, that it was a pity so many magnificent skins should be tacked around the walls, and
lying on the floor, just for ornament, when there
are enough there to make us all a set of winter
furs. He said he would send them off in a few
days, so I think you will have your wish gratified
before long."

The boys were sent with the wagon to bring
back the meat of the two cows that Joe had
killed, and about noon they returned. The
robes were very fine ones. Joe asked the Pawnees to tan them for him, and when they were
finished, which would be in about a week, he
intended to make them a present to his father
and mother for their bedroom.

The buffalo meat was cut up that evening, by
Mr. Thompson, and on the next day was smoked
with corn-cobs, which are always used for that
purpose out West.

While getting the meat ready, Mr. Thompson

told the boys that he wouldn't be at all surprised
if, when they wanted buffalo again, they would
have to go miles away for them, as the country
was becoming so thickly settled that the herds
might never come as far east as the Oxhide.
" Of course," continued he, " the antelope will
remain with us a long time yet, but even they
will become scarcer each year, and then they,
too, will disappear, for it seems that the great
ruminants of the plains cannot live with the
white man as they can with the savages. The
latter have no permanent home, but congregate
in temporary villages in the winter, and as soon
as spring opens, they are off again, living on
horseback and depending upon the chase for
their existence. It has ever been so with the
Indian since the landing of the Pilgrims, in
1620. The white man has dogged their footsteps
as they themselves follow the deer. One of the
facetious old bishops of New England, I forgot
his name now, said: ' The Puritans, when they
landed on Plymouth Rock, first fell upon *their
knees*, and then upon the *aboriginees!* ' It ap-
pears to be the fate of the red men to vanish
before the onward march of the whites."

" I feel sorry for the Indians, father," said Joe. " I tell you it would have made you almost weep to hear White Wolf, that night we camped on the Walnut, relate in his sorrowful manner how powerful his tribe once was, before the white man took their lands away from them."

" I have a warm spot in my heart for the Indian," said Mr. Thompson, "but it is their fate, I suppose, and cannot be helped. You cannot civilize the old ones, and the only hope is in taking the rising generation away from their tribal affiliations when young, and teaching them to live like the whites."

CHAPTER XIX

THE INDIAN HORSE-RACE — KATE'S PONY WINS — THE TRADE WITH
THE PAWNEES — THE DANCES AT NIGHT — THE INDIANS SAY
GOOD BY TO THE FAMILY — NOBLE ACTION OF WHITE WOLF

THE Pawnees having remained on the Oxhide
much longer than in any previous season, they
began to make preparations for departure. Joe
asked the chief to give a dance with his warriors
at the ranche, for his parents and his sisters to
see how the Indians enjoy themselves.

White Wolf said he would be sure to do so
the night before they left. To-morrow, they were
going to have a horse-race, and, should his father
be willing, they would use that long, level stretch
of prairie between the house and the creek. It
was a distance of about four miles, the usual
length of a race-course with the Indians.

White Wolf said that the wagers would be ten
horses, and that if Young Panther wanted to bet,
he would make one with him. Joe replied that
neither he nor his father approved of betting, but

that both of them dearly loved to see horses run. " If I believed in betting, though," said Joe to the chief, " I would bet that my sister's pony, Ginger, can outrun any pony you have." The chief smiled, and told Joe that if he would not bet, he might ride that pony in the race, and if he came out ahead, then he would know whether his sister's animal was the fastest. Joe agreed to it, and when he returned to Errolstrath he obtained Kate's permission to ride Ginger in the race the following day. Mr. Thompson had readily given his consent to the Indians to use the trail in front of the house as a race-course.

Joe went down to the camp that evening and told the warriors that they might have the use of the course. White Wolf then said: " We will be up there by the time the sun is so high," pointing with his hand to where the sun would be at eight o'clock.

" All right," replied Joe; " we will be ready for you. The folks can sit on the porch and see the whole length of the course. Be sure to come promptly."

When Joe returned to the ranche, he announced that he wanted to get up very early in the morning, and as Rob was always the first one in the house out of bed, he asked him to call him the moment he awoke.

Rob, as usual, was out before sunrise. He promptly called his brother, who lost no time in dressing, washing at the spring, and going out to the pasture to catch Ginger. He led him to the corral, gave him a most vigorous currying, after which he fed the pony an extra ration of oats, to give him heart for the race.

Shortly after breakfast was out of the way, Kate, who was on the veranda, feeding the mocking-birds, came rushing into the sitting-room, crying, " The Pawnees are coming; I can hear their tom-toms beating; they will soon be here!"

All the family went out, and sure enough, there were the Indians all dressed up in feathers, and painted in every imaginable savage manner. White Wolf had a row of white dots on one cheek, flanked on each side by a streak of vermilion, while the other was green and blue. He had on a war bonnet with eagle feathers sticking in it around the upper edge, making it look like a grotesque crown. Down his back dragged a long trail of buffalo hair plaited into his own, and at every few inches for its whole length (it reached the ground when he walked) there were fastened bright metal disks nearly as big as the top of a tomato can. Around his wrists were a dozen or more brass rings, and on his bare ankles he wore as many rings of the same material. He had an embroidered buffalo robe thrown gracefully over his shoulders, half concealing his coat of beaded buckskin. His leggings were of the same stuff, and were also gayly decorated with colored porcupine quills deftly woven in them. The other warriors were similarly dressed and painted, but wore only one eagle feather in their bonnets, which was the distinguishing feature between them and their chief.

Following the warriors were the boys of the band, each riding a pony, and leading others which had been wagered on the race.

The race animals were ridden by their owners, and came after all the others; among them was the wild coal-black stallion that White Wolf had captured on the Cimarron. He looked like himself now, as he proudly pranced along, his mouth frothing as he champed on his rawhide bit, and his neck arched as he stepped like a thorough-bred over buffalo-grass turf leading to the house.

Several of the warriors had tom-toms in front of them, which they were beating vigorously with a stick as they rode proudly along. The tom-toms, or drums, are made of tanned buffalo hide stretched over a willow hoop, and the sound resembles that of a drum, but as the pounding is simply a continuous series of strokes without any variation, it is not music, but a very monotonous noise.

When the band had arrived at the house the Indians dismounted, and after a series of " Hows? " — their customary salutation — to the family on the veranda, they dismounted and began to converse among themselves in an excited manner. Presently one of the warriors started on a run toward the creek. He soon returned with some sticks, and then he and another warrior began to mark out the course.

This took them some time, and while they were at the work, the boys who were to ride the race began to cinch up their buffalo-hide saddles, and prepare themselves for the impending struggle.

Joe was already prancing about on Ginger, and he could hardly hold the spirited little beast, so anxious was it to be off, as if it perfectly understood the meaning of all the preparations. The Indian ponies, too, seemed to enter into the spirit of the thing, for they also commenced to cavort around, and it was with much difficulty that their riders could restrain them from bolting down the track.

At last everything was in readiness, the animals in place, Joe on the outside of the four who were to run. The animals were all jumping up and down, stiff-legged, and bucking with all their strength to throw their riders.

In a few moments White Wolf gave the signal, and away they darted like meteors. Ginger kept his place well, the black stallion leading for the first half-mile until a big roan of one of the warriors took the lead; then Ginger made a dash ahead. For a moment it was nip and tuck which would keep the lead, but when the second mile was half run, the animals began to show their powers of endurance. Some flagged, others were far behind, and Ginger and the roan were going relatively slower;

when all at once, just as the home stretch was reached, Ginger took a spurt and seeming to gain his second wind, like a pugilist in the ring, came in forty feet in advance of the roan, the black stallion twenty feet behind him. The other ponies were so far away, that if they had been running on a white man's course they would have been declared "distanced."

Such a shout went up from the veranda of the house, where the family were sitting, as they saw Ginger dash ahead, and Joe caught the sound of it as the wind wafted the pæan of victory to his ears.

White Wolf was disappointed in the result. He thought that his black horse had great powers of endurance, and as soon as they were assembled in front of the veranda, he offered Kate five of the best and youngest of his horses in exchange for Ginger. Kate hesitated for a moment, but considering that Ginger was now nearly eight years old, and after consulting with her father and Joe, she decided to make the swap.

As the chief owned the roan that had really won the race, — Ginger being a mere outsider

just to test Joe's belief that he was the fastest
animal, — White Wolf was, in fact, the winner,
and took the ten ponies that were wagered.

With the assistance of her father and brothers,
Kate selected five of the best and youngest of
the chief's bunch, including the roan. The Indians then returned to their camp, promising
to come up that evening and give a series of
dances, as they intended to start for their reservation the next morning.

After they had left the front of the house,
and Joe had taken the five new ponies to the
corral, he told Kate that he would now let her
have Cheyenne back, and he would take the
roan, as the latter was too large a horse for her
to ride. Kate agreed readily to the proposition,
so she once more owned the little animal that had
brought her so safely from the Indian village.

When the family had finished their supper,
Joe and Rob, with a team of work horses,
dragged several large logs from the creek to
the front of the house to make a big bonfire,
for the Pawnee dance.

Shortly after dark the redskins came up
with their best toggery on, and when Joe, who

had donned his Indian suit for the occasion, told White Wolf he was ready, the Indians commenced to circle around the great fire of logs, in their savage fashion. Some of them jumped stiff-legged like an antelope when he is first startled. Others, bending nearly double, shuffled in pairs, each one on his own hook, trying to see which could make the most ridiculous postures, for they have no regular figures, but keep admirable time to the drumming on the tom-toms.

When the first dance was finished, they gave a representation of the scalp dance. The chief crept along the ground, putting his ear close to it, in the attitude of listening on the trail of the enemy, then waving his hand for his warriors to come on, they rushed into a supposed Indian camp, and went through the simulation of killing their victim, and wrenching off his hair with their knives. The motions, which at times were really graceful, were carried on in perfect unison with the monotonous pounding of the drums.

The next dance was named " Make the buffalo come." The medicine-men, who claim to possess mysterious powers, tell the warriors to dance, for

that will make the buffalo come, and then they
can get their meat.   The crafty old fellows are
sure never to order the dance until about the
season that the animals come to that part of the
country where the tribe may happen to be.   They
are kept dancing night after night until the buffalo really make their appearance, then the medicine-men claim that they brought them by their
incantations and the wonderful power of their
medicine.

For this dance, White Wolf's warriors and himself covered their heads with the skin of a buffalo's head, horns and all, so that they looked like
a lot of men with the heads of that animal as part
of their anatomy.   It was a long dance, and during its performance, the most indescribable antics
were gone through.

The family were well pleased with the entertainment, and when it was over, Mrs. Thompson
invited the Indians into the sitting-room, where
the girls had prepared a little supper for them,
consisting of cake and lemonade.   The latter was
new, and created quite a sensation, but Joe told
them it was not fire-water, and they might drink
a barrel full without becoming crazy.

At midnight when the dances and the supper were over, the Pawnees rode back to their camp, delighted with their evening's entertainment.

The next morning Joe was down at the Indian camp very early to see his dusky friends make ready for their departure. The chief told him that they had camped on the Oxhide for the last time; the whites had taken up all the country, and the buffalo would come there no more. Now when they needed buffalo meat, they would be obliged to go out as far as the Walnut, and in a few more years there would be no buffalo at all. His people would have to take the " white man's road" if they expected to live. He and the other warriors made their youthful friend some presents, and told him that they had to go by the house to take the trail down the Smoky Hill Fork to their distant home. He said that they would stop a moment at the ranche to say good by to all the people who had been so kind to him and the tribe every year since they had camped on the creek.

Joe returned to Errolstrath, feeling very sad, because he had become much attached to the Indians, and he knew that he would miss them so much, and feel lonely for a long time. He told the family that the Pawnees would come soon to say farewell, and that they must be sure to be out on the veranda when they came.

By nine o'clock, Kate, whose ears were well trained to faint sounds, through her vigilance when a captive in the Cheyenne camp, came into the house from the porch where she had been attending to her birds as usual, and said the Pawnees were coming; she could hear the tread of their ponies' hoofs.

Then the family took their places on the veranda, as they had promised Joe. Presently, slowly coming up the trail, with White Wolf in the lead, the band of Pawnees were seen approaching the house. Arrived in front, they all halted, and with their usual "How? How?" saluted the family.

All came down from the porch to shake hands, when Ginger, who with the other ponies was running loose in the bunch, came up to Kate and, neighing affectionately, began to rub his nose against her arm and shoulder. The salutation of her once favorite pony was too much for the warm-hearted girl, and she burst into tears as she returned the animal's love for her by throwing her arms around his neck.

"Oh, father!" said she, "why did I ever consent to part with Ginger? I am so sorry now. I would give worlds to have him back again."

White Wolf, noticing her weeping, asked in his own language why the little squaw was feeling so badly. Joe told him how she loved Ginger and how sorry she was she had ever consented to give him up.

White Wolf then said: "Tell her she shall have her pony again. I am a chief and do not like to see the white squaws cry." He dismounted from his animal, and going up to Kate, took Ginger's foretop in his hand; then taking hers, he pressed into it the bunch of hair.

Ginger neighed when the rude ceremony of returning him to his former mistress was over, seeming to understand just what had been effected.

Kate took the chief by the hand and thanked him as earnestly as she could find language to express herself, which, of course, had to be interpreted by Joe.

Then Rob brought from the stable the five

other ponies that had been given for Ginger, and after a few more parting salutations the Pawnees rode down the trail.

Ginger was restored to his stall in the stable, and Kate was the happiest girl in the settlement that day.

CHAPTER XX

RETROSPECTIVE — THE OLD TRAPPER PASSES AWAY — MR. AND
MRS. THOMPSON ARE DEAD — GENERAL CUSTER AND COLONEL
KEOGH ARE KILLED — ERROLSTRATH BELONGS TO JOE AND
ROB

TWENTY-NINE years have elapsed since the
events related in this story. The Indians, buffalo, and antelope have all disappeared. There
is no longer any frontier. Granite monuments
mark the dividing line between great states.
The children of this generation will never know
by experience the hardships, the perils, and the
amusements which so conspicuously characterized the life of Joe, Rob, Gertrude, and Kate at
Errolstrath.

General Custer, Colonel Keogh, and nearly all
of the famous cavalry regiment commanded by
the great Indian fighter went down to their
death in the awful massacre at the battle of the

Little Bighorn, or Rosebud, as it is sometimes called.

The old trapper, Mr. Tucker, who was such a warm friend of the family, has long since passed away. Mr. and Mrs. Thompson are buried in the quiet cemetery on the hill, near the ranche. Kate and her sister have been married for many years and still live in Kansas, but not at the dear old home. Errolstrath belongs to Joe and Rob. It is now a large ranche, comprising many thousand acres. Where the buffalo and the antelope used to roam in such vast herds are to be seen, peacefully grazing, hundreds of mild-eyed Jerseys and the broad-backed Durhams. A new house with all modern improvements has been erected on the site of the old one. On its broad veranda may be seen every evening in summer the children of the two brothers, to whom, as the shadows lengthen, they tell of their own early experiences when they too were children and when the ranche was far out in the wilderness of the great central plains.

The shrill whistle of the locomotive may be heard at the ranche as the palace trains with their load of living freight dash along the bank of the

Smoky Hill, toward the Rocky Mountains. Ellsworth has grown to be a beautiful town with electric lights and all the appliances of our wonderful nineteenth century civilization.

The moon shines as brightly and the birds sing as sweetly as of yore around Errolstrath, but of all the familiar faces that knew it so many years ago, only those of Joe and Rob may be seen. Even they are bearded, their hair is slightly mixed with gray. They are growing old; but the laughter of their merry children serves to keep green the memory of their own happy childhood.

THE OLD SANTA FÉ TRAIL.

COLONEL HENRY INMAN.

8vo.   Cloth. $3.50.

Preface by Col. W. F. CODY (Buffalo Bill).   Eight full-page repro-
ductions in photogravure of Illustrations by FREDERIC REMING-
TON.   Initials, Tailpieces, etc., in the text, comprising portraits
of famous Indians, scouts, trappers, etc., points of special interest on the Trail, etc.

PRESS COMMENTS.

From the *New York Tribune :*

"Colonel Inman's recollections cover a period of more than thirty years.
For events of the earlier part of the century he has been able to draw upon
reminiscences of comrades who had themselves participated in them.   Hence
his book is authentic in its data, and presents a picture of the Old Santa Fé
Trail which lacks nothing of verisimilitude and burning color.   He has, too, a
straightforward and persuasive style.   No better historian of his subject could
have been chosen. . . .   Starting out to write a history of the Santa Fé Trail
from just before the time in the early twenties when wagon trains took the place
of pack mules, Colonel Inman tries to be historical and consecutive, but he soon
yields to the temptation to drop into plainsman's yarns, and to write as though
he were amusing the listeners around a camp-fire.   It is not in the least to his
discredit.   The book is better for its informality. . .   The main point is that
Colonel Inman is unfailingly graphic and stirring, that he revives indubitable
pictures of the old trail that is now no more than a memory, and he brings once
more upon the scene the Indians and Indian fighters, the red warriors and white
captives, the picturesque old stage coaches, the scouts, trappers, teamsters, mur-
derers and other desperadoes who belong to the romantic era of our history.
For that and for the excellent illustrations to his story let us be thankful."

MRS. LILIAN WHITING in *The Inter-Ocean,* Chicago:

"That truth is stranger than fiction is attested by the extraordinary developments of that new book by Colonel Henry Inman, 'The Old Santa Fé Trail,'
giving the story of a great highway.   Here is a detective romance, a sensational
novel, a story as startling in its developments as is Irving's play 'The Lyons
Mail,' and yet a part of the history of our own country. . . .   The story of this
old highway is a chapter in American history of the most romantic interest.
The contrast of the life in the decade of 1830–40 to that of 1890–1900 in our
country is something beyond imagination."

THE MACMILLAN COMPANY,
66 Fifth Avenue, New York.

ON MANY SEAS.

THE LIFE AND EXPLOITS OF A YANKEE SAILOR.

BY

HERBERT ELLIOTT HAMBLEN.

EDITED BY HIS FRIEND

WILLIAM STONE BOOTH.

12mo. Cloth. $1.50.

COMMENTS OF THE PRESS.

" Every line of this hits the mark, and to anyone who knows the forecastle and its types the picture appeals with the urgency of old familiar things. All through his four hundred and more pages he is equally unaffected and forcible, equally picturesque. To go through one chapter is to pass with lively anticipation to the next. His book is destined to be remembered."— *New York Tribune.*

"The book reads like a romance, but is at the same time realistic history, before which the fancy ships and the fancy sailors of the novelist are pale and faded."

— *Baltimore Sun.*

"The charm of the book is its simplicity and truth. The author, as I happen to know, can spin thrilling yarns by the hour, and this book of his is simply one long yarn of his life. A seaman every inch of him, he writes as only a sailor can. No landsman, no amateur yachtsman, could write a book like this. The entire book bears the stamp of truth, and in this age of literary shams that is a crowning merit."— *New York Herald.*

THE MACMILLAN COMPANY,

66 Fifth Avenue, New York.

YANKEE SHIPS AND YANKEE SAILORS: Tales of 1812.

BY

JAMES BARNES,

Author of "Naval Engagements of the War of 1812."
" A Loyal Traitor," " For King and Country," etc.

**With Numerous Illustrations by R. F. ZOGBAUM and
CARLTON T. CHAPMAN.**

Crown 8vo.   Cloth, gilt top. $1.50.

COMMENTS.

" 'There are passages in this book which are as strong
and captivating as the work of the best writers of the
day; to mariners and those who love the sea and ships
these tales will appeal irresistibly.

" Each story is a gem by itself.   It is told with a direct-
ness and a strength which carries conviction.   All are
based upon actual occurrences, Mr. Barnes tells us, and
while some of the incidents related may come under the
head of tradition, yet most of them are historical facts, and
he has worked up each tale so cleverly, so compactly, so
entertainingly, that they may, one and all, be taken for
models of their kind." — *Seaboard.*

" Good stories well told are those of 'Yankee Ships and
Yankee Sailors.'   They deal with the gallant defenders of
such vessels as the *Chesapeake*, the *Vixen*, the fiery little
Wasp, and grand ' *Old Ironsides*.'   All the stories are
told in a spirited style that will quicken the blood and the
love of country in every Yankee heart."
— New England Magazine.

THE MACMILLAN COMPANY,

66 Fifth Avenue, New York.

2

www.ingramcontent.com/pod-product-compliance
Lightning Source LLC
Chambersburg PA
CBHW060520030726
47498CB00004B/1008